The Architect

ALSO BY JOHN SCOTT

Selected Poems (1968–90)
Blair
What I Have Written
Before I Wake

JOHN SCOTT

THE ARCHITECT

A TALE

VIKING

Viking
Penguin Books Australia Ltd
487 Maroondah Highway, PO Box 257
Ringwood, Victoria 3134, Australia
Penguin Books Ltd
Harmondsworth, Middlesex, England
Penguin Putnam Inc.
375 Hudson Street, New York, New York 10014, USA
Penguin Books Canada Limited
10 Alcorn Avenue, Toronto, Ontario, Canada M4V 3B2
Penguin Books (NZ) Ltd
Cnr Rosedale and Airborne Roads, Albany, Auckland, New Zealand
Penguin Books (South Africa) (Pty) Ltd
5 Watkins Street, Denver Ext 4, 2094, South Africa
Penguin Books India (P) Ltd
11, Community Centre, Panchsheel Park, New Delhi 110 017, India

First published by Penguin Books Australia Ltd 2001

1 3 5 7 9 10 8 6 4 2

Copyright © John Scott 2001

The moral right of the author has been asserted

All rights reserved. Without limiting the rights under copyright reserved above,
no part of this publication may be reproduced, stored in or introduced into
a retrieval system, or transmitted, in any form or by any means (electronic,
mechanical, photocopying, recording or otherwise), without the prior written
permission of both the copyright owner and the above publisher of this book.

Jacket and pages designed by Nikki Townsend, Penguin Design Studio
Typeset in Apollo MT 11.25/16.5 by Midland Typesetters, Maryborough, Victoria
Made and printed in Australia by Australian Print Group, Maryborough, Victoria

National Library of Australia
Cataloguing-in-Publication data:

Scott, John A., 1948– .
The architect.

ISBN 0 670 91044 9.

I. Title.

A823.3

www.penguin.com.au

For Elizabeth Francis and John Hughes

Shall mortal man be more just than God?
Shall a man be more pure than his maker?

Job 4: 17

prologue

Johannes Von Ruhland approached the long mirror at the passageway's end. He smiled to himself.

'Where have you been?' he asked.

'Walking through the streets.'

'Did you see him? How unique he is? How perfect?'

'Yes, I saw him.'

'How loving.'

'You are certain?'

'Yes. *Völlig.*'

'Totally?'

'Meaning?'

'He has everything. I wonder, though, if you should somehow touch his life . . .'

Von Ruhland paused a moment. A brief flash of doubt crossed his face, then he added decisively:

'Touch him.'

1

That the young architect had been invited to Berlin had come as a surprise to no-one. Though only in his early thirties, he was acknowledged as a major innovator in the field of waterfront development, the subject of the *Wasserstadt Berlin* conference.

Andrew Martin's friends and associates had come that evening to his inner-city apartment to celebrate and to wish him *bon voyage*, amongst them his business partner Alex Jacobs, the architect Gavin Belsey, and Natalie Vlies, landscape designer. Shortly before eight o'clock these three found themselves in a close group drinking champagne with Martin's wife, Sara.

'The old buildings exist,' she was saying. 'They're waiting for a vision. Not that anything's simple – they're deep and large, so how do you get light into them? And then there are the usual problems with waterfronts: the ground's badly polluted with heavy metals and oil.'

'Not to mention the changing water tables,' Jacobs added, prodding his glasses back on the bridge of his nose.

'I take it Andrew's being as conciliatory as ever,' said Belsey, who had already drunk too much.

Sara smiled. 'Let's just say he starts out by suggesting

so far they've got it completely wrong – architects have become building designers. Andrew's asking how you can build on the concept of the construction site itself.'

'Mind you, Berlin's built on sand, and you know what the Bible has to say about that,' Belsey replied, turning to Natalie Vlies. 'Could you be a dear and pass me that rather nice Billecart.' He took the bottle in his hand. 'I'm wondering if he'll bump into his idol at this conference.'

'Von what's-his-name, do you mean?' Jacobs enquired. 'I thought he died years ago.' He turned towards the selection of tapas laid out on a nearby table.

'Now that you mention it, I think you may be right,' said Belsey, largely to himself, passing back the champagne and taking a quick mouthful from his brimming flute. His gaze slid a moment from the group, fortuitously catching Martin moving from his daughter's bedroom on the mezzanine.

'Ah!' Belsey announced. 'Hail the conquering hero comes!'

Martin walked down the stairway into the central room, his arrival met with applause from the assembled guests. Belsey nudged forward through the group, holding out his hand to the young architect.

'You know,' he said, 'and I don't care about admitting it here in public, I envy you, Andrew. It's not everyone who gets invited to tell the Germans what they should do with their new capital.'

'Yes, congratulations, Andrew,' said Natalie, stepping forward to kiss him on the cheek.

'How's Naomi?' asked Sara.

'"Hansel and Gretel" again. The witch went in the oven three times.'

'She'll have nightmares. If she's up during the night, *you're* going, overseas flight or not.'

'I think we should all drink a toast to our very clever Andrew Martin,' Natalie announced.

'I'll second that!' called Jacobs, raising a Spanish meatball on a toothpick.

'Here's to Andrew,' Natalie continued. 'Internationally acclaimed architect, most likely to succeed, and a pretty nice guy as well.'

Sara glanced back from Natalie to Martin and found for a short moment a reluctance to join in the toast, not because of the praise to her husband, whom she loved and to whom praise was undoubtedly due, but on account of its proposer and the style of its proposition.

'To Andrew,' they all said.

Eyes closed, Martin listened to the still steady hum from the city bypass. A screech of tyres jolted him from his reverie. He glanced at his watch: midnight, and the last of the guests, Belsey, had not long been ushered into a taxi. Martin looked up from the balcony, across the wing of the angelic figure of *Fortuna*, the Corlett sculpture that stood watch outside his apartment. The shadowed roofing of the nearby Victoria Market set forth the frozen ripple of its corrugation.

Sara's voice emerged from the silence behind him.

'She fancies you.'

Martin half turned from the balcony railing and met her eyes.

'The angel?'

'You know exactly who I mean,' she said, adding the name for emphasis, not for any reason of clarification: 'Natalie.'

'Well, she can't have me. I'm well and truly taken.' And he moved to her, closing her in his arms.

'You should get some sleep,' said Sara.

'I'll sleep on the plane.'

'You never sleep on planes.'

'That's because I always get a good night's sleep beforehand. See, you have an obligation to keep me awake for at least another hour.'

They walked together back inside the apartment, the young architect and his wife.

2 Berlin that late September was a collection of greys. The slate-grey of cobblestones. Buildings the grey of dead wood, the grey of dust. The very air seemed bleached by mist, the distance lost; the perspective, to Martin, staring from his window at the Kempinski, seemed flattened. Two-dimensional. Berlin was a photograph.

He moved back into the room and took a seat in an armchair. For the first time since his arrival three days before, he could afford to relax. All things considered, his contribution to *Wasserstadt Berlin* had been a grand success. The conference paper had been delivered and had, as anticipated, provoked the audience into equally animated praise and condemnation. Martin had found his name occurring in otherwise incomprehensible German sentences. At a dinner, an architect had referred to 'the Martin position'.

The conference materials were now gathered together in a neat pile at one side of the desk. Martin's gaze fell upon the program, the cover design with its borrowing from the 1954 film poster: *On the Waterfront*. *Wasserstadt Berlin: Potentiale, Standorte, Visionen*. There was little in its remaining days of interest to him. Now he could declare himself a tourist, ambling unrecognised through the streets. He would venture forth tomorrow and buy gifts. Within forty-eight hours the whole thing would be over and he would be flying back to his wife and daughter.

Martin reached to the small pile of books he had purchased that afternoon at a visual arts bookshop beneath the overhead rail line at Savignyplatz Station, edging out an exhibition catalogue of Peter Zumthor's *Three Concepts*. He turned slowly through the plans: the thermal bath at Vals, the Bregenz art museum, the 'Topography of Terror'.

With the latter he had some familiarity. In Berlin, set amongst the ruined buildings which had previously housed the SS, the SD, the Gestapo, had been a temporary exhibition of photographs and documents chronicling the rise of the Nazi regime. In the early 1990s a competition was held for the design of a permanent structure to house these materials. It had been won by Peter Zumthor, his vision based on the concept of enclosing the ruins in an architectural envelope. A building which would speak no language other than that of the material itself, its construction and its unique function.

Martin skipped through the catalogue to the reproductions of Zumthor's models. He found a skeletal building with closely aligned prefabricated concrete bars, a form in which nothing was concealed – every structural sin clearly visible – standing between two flanking piles of rubble.

From outside his room came a brisk knock. Martin slipped a sheet of hotel notepaper between the pages of the book, and calling out, 'One moment,' the Englishness of the words striking him instantly, moved to the door. By the time he opened it, however, there was no-one to be seen. Only to his left, where the corridor led to the lifts, could he sense a disturbance of air, a trace of heat perhaps – the attributes of a recent vanishing. It was then he saw the envelope bearing his name on the floor at his feet. Bending down to pick it up he noticed, only a metre or so away, on the blue carpet with its pattern of criss-cross lines, a single off-white feather, softly plumed, presumably dropped in the wake of the cleaners.

Weighing the envelope in his hand, he closed the door and moved to the desk where he manoeuvred the hotel pencil into the flap, tearing the envelope open, ringleting its top edge. He unfolded the thick letter paper which bore, he remarked, an embossed address in Fasanenstrasse.

At first sight he thought the message to be in German, written as it was in old gothic script.

Dear Mr Martin,

May I take this opportunity of welcoming you to Berlin and of adding my voice to the concert of praise for your achievements? As fate has decreed you are staying in the very same street as myself, I was wondering whether, time of course permitting, you might consent to paying me a brief visit? Tomorrow afternoon, around three o'clock, would be perfect. Please feel under no obligation to reply – if it is possible, simply arrive; if not, I have much work with which to continue.

I remain yours sincerely,
Johannes Von Ruhland

Martin stared at the brief letter and the signature below: it was little less than a visitation. To the young Australian architect, Von Ruhland had long been an object of fascination. From his mid-teens onward he had sought out information on the man, an engrossment kindled, he well knew, by the passing mention of 'an unacknowledged genius' in the postwar diaries of Douglas Stewart, a leather-bound volume left open in the family library. He could still see the page with the architect's name faintly underlined in pencil, as though it had been offered as a thread to be followed through the labyrinthine shadows occasioned by his father's sudden death, as though an invitation to a voyage his father may himself have wished to take. Johannes Von Ruhland, architect: whose name would surface in the correspondence of poets and musicians. Here a dedication – 'To JVR, who teaches us' – from Orff; here an acknowledgment in the later notebooks of Vlaminck; here a simple exclamatory mention in the margin of a Heidegger manuscript. And what of Mann's attempt at describing the building he had briefly glimpsed one evening as a sketch upon a drawing board before an intervening door had closed against it? A description, he would go on to assert, which served only to demonstrate the impoverishment of his own artistry.

For over half his years, this gleaning. And what he found were little more than shreds of a life and its work, passing allusions that only bolstered a sense of a visionary, rendering his obscurity a taste more bitter in the mouth.

Nor in recent times, it should be said, had Martin's interest in the man abated. Only the previous year he had prepared a lengthy article for *Blueprint*, an exploration of how absence could be seen to shape what is present, in particular how an architect, no building of whose survived, might be seen as capable of influencing the design of so many buildings.

Martin sat on the bed, bolstered by the pillows in their striped damask casings. He was waiting for eight o'clock, the hour he knew to be the earliest he could reasonably ring his wife. From the muted television poured images of the forthcoming national election – the concerned or confident politicians, the diagrams labelled with meaningless acronyms: FDP, SPD, PDS, CDU/CSU.

The anchorwoman reappeared on the screen and Martin glanced down at his watch. He leaned across to the bedside table, bringing first the telephone then the letter from Von Ruhland to his lap. The second hand swept across the 12 and he lifted the receiver.

The young architect telephoned his wife – herself only recently arisen on the following day – barely uttering the words 'Hello, how are you? And Naomi?' before embarking upon the substance of this recent correspondence.

3 Martin, his black three-quarter coat unbuttoned, strode down Fasanenstrasse with its slowly unleaving trees, heading south, crossing Ku'damm, passing the Käthe Kollwitz Museum, occasionally forced wide on the footpaths where the small cobblestone blocks bit at the soles of his feet. He carried Von Ruhland's letter with him, placing in his present state of mind little trust in his memory, but also by way of admission that part of him expected no meeting to occur – that a door would simply open to a stranger and this piece of paper would be his sole defence against their suspicions or accusations.

He paused at the small but densely treed park which was Fasanenplatz and consulted the address a final time. It summoned him to a five-storey block of nineteenth-century apartments directly ahead. As he approached,

Martin picked out a small number of details: the turreted corners, the elaborate pediments around the windows, a frieze running below the top two floors depicting a hare fleeing a pack of hounds, whilst a second watched from its hiding place behind a thick bush.

Shortly before three o'clock, Martin entered the foyer of the building and climbed the staircase to the top floor. He removed the letter once again from his pocket, holding it at the ready, and knocked.

When the door opened, Martin found himself before a tall and still handsome man in his mid-seventies, his hair closely cropped, his skin quite deeply tanned. Martin stood there staring at the face of this man whose likeness he had sought these seventeen years, for throughout the length of his enquiries, he had never uncovered an image of the architect himself.

'Mr Martin,' Von Ruhland announced with absolute certainty. 'I am so pleased you were able to visit.' And he stood aside to let the younger architect enter.

'You are not a smoking man?' Von Ruhland asked.

'No,' Martin said, immediately disarmed by the question.

'No. So few are these days. You see, this apartment is equipped with a smoking room.' He gestured to his right and slowly shook his head. 'I have often been encouraged to take up the habit simply because an area has been designated for the purpose.'

Von Ruhland ushered Martin into an adjoining room, a dark and ornately wallpapered space overburdened with bourgeois possessions – figurative ornaments, a bust, brooding seascapes, a bearskin rug.

'The *Salon*,' he announced. 'Please, take a seat.'

He waited for Martin to choose a place, then sat himself.

'It interests me, the designation of rooms in domestic architecture, the manner in which it shapes our behaviours. The Bauhaus, of course, drew up a list of twelve motives when building a house. If my memory serves me well, the first three were sex life, sleeping habits and pets. Socialising was not amongst the twelve, but here, in the *Salon*, you are most welcome.'

'I'm really honoured,' said Martin, conscious of his mouth already dry with fear.

'The feeling is quite mutual,' Von Ruhland replied. 'I have always maintained a vigorous interest in the future. You, Mr Martin, are part of this. A most important and exciting part. This is an age of ideas and we will not be moved by architecture that doesn't offer solutions to conceptual problems.'

'Thank you, Herr Von Ruhland,' Martin began, ready to qualify what he saw as an overly generous assessment.

'Johannes, please.'

'Then Andrew,' he said, offering his name to the architect. 'You must call me Andrew.'

'Well now, Andrew, I am making coffee. Would you care for some?'

'This is not your first visit to Berlin.' Von Ruhland placed the *Espresso Tasse* on the table next to Martin's chair.

'Thanks,' said Martin, touching the saucer slightly as if to acknowledge its presence. 'I was here for a couple of days last year. We had some business with a German company – Bauwelt. You would know it.'

'To be sure.'

'But I've been following the development of Potsdamer Platz for some time on the Internet.'

'The Cityscope site,' said Von Ruhland, settling back into his chair.

Martin nodded.

'So, what have you made of our city? Apart from your merciless denunciations of the waterfront developments!'

Martin went to defend himself as someone who had abused another's hospitality by an ungracious remark.

'Don't take me the wrong way, Andrew,' Von Ruhland reassured. 'I can only agree with you. However, I would not stop at the waterfront. How does the average Berliner refer to our recent architectural efforts? "The lipstick" and "the powderbox", "the armadillo"; indeed, "the pregnant oyster", which played host to your conference. They have already passed judgment on these piecemeal offerings. So please, speak freely.'

'It strikes me as a place still searching for an identity,' said Martin, immediately conscious of his statement's generality.

Von Ruhland waited a moment.

'You mentioned the Cityscope site before,' he eventually replied. 'Over a hundred years ago, the novelist

Alberti was marvelling at the vast construction site near Potsdamer Platz with all its cranes and its workmen and its piles of rubble. One of our problems is that the city has never been finished. We've seen a parade of visions inevitably falling to the destruction of war. It is a truism that Berlin has always been in a state of *becoming*.'

Von Ruhland took a breath of sufficient depth to suggest he was savouring the air of the *Salon*.

'What intrigues me is why there is a city here at all,' he continued. 'There is no landmark of significance, no port, no mountain, no great river. There are no natural resources, only a random mark on a vast swamp-ridden plain, bitterly cold and inhospitable.'

He paused a moment to take a sip of his coffee. 'Berlin arises only from an effort of will to create it.'

'You have visited the Reichstag?'

'I've seen photos of the conversion.'

'Sir Norman's overly large cupola – the "English egg" as they say – has little interest to me. It is that *other* architecture which captures my imagination. You are aware they have recently uncovered more tunnels? A virtual labyrinth beneath the building, spreading out Heaven knows where.'

Von Ruhland lifted the *Espresso Tasse* and studied the coffee grains in the bottom of the cup, then looked up at Martin.

'It would not surprise me were they to find an entire city beneath Berlin – the streets narrow and flooded in black water – where people had shaped another destiny for themselves quite independently of us.'

Martin caught his own reflection in the mirrored front of a dresser. He corrected the slight slouch he discovered in his posture.

'What did Nietzsche say of the German soul?' Von Ruhland continued. 'That it has corridors, interconnecting corridors. That there are caves, hiding places and dungeons in it.'

He placed his cup back on its saucer. 'The German is acquainted with the hidden paths to chaos.'

4 Martin could see the light outside quickly fading. He realised his time with the older architect was rapidly coming to an end. Any moment now it would be necessary for him to stand and take his leave. He would carry from this meeting little more than a small bundle of opinions, broad strokes of appreciation or of criticism, words that might serve as dinner-party conversation, but nothing of substance. He felt no closer to knowing this man – his opportunity had largely been squandered by his own reticence, his overawed procession of single sentences.

'So, what are your plans after the conference?' Von Ruhland was asking.

'A return flight to Australia.'

'You are leaving so soon! Are there pressing needs which demand your return?'

'Nothing urgent,' Martin began.

'Then you should think of staying on for a few days more. Even a week.'

'I'm not sure the budget would stretch to –'

'But here, you must stay *here*.' Von Ruhland spread wide his arms as if to encompass the entire apartment. 'I have so much space and so little use for it to be put!' He took a breath in which Martin made no reply. 'My offer is not totally selfless,' he added, sensing the younger man's opposition had begun to fade. 'Who, these days, will talk to an aging architect? Your presence here would bring me so much pleasure.'

Ku'damm that September evening was vibrant. Perhaps, it passed through Martin's mind, this was the way it would have been in its heyday in the 1920s. It drew him away from the path to his hotel; it led him past the indefatigable restaurant touters, past the newspaper stalls and the pooling bus queues approaching Joachimstaler Strasse; it led him past the Café Kranzler, onwards to the gaping floodlit church of Kaiser Wilhelm.

On the way back to the hotel he stopped to eat at Moevenpick. He wished to contemplate his recent good fortune, and the anonymity of the large self-serve restaurant suited him well. For his celebratory dinner he chose two chicken legs, a medium-sized plate of vegetables and a small glass of red wine – the entire meal costing him under fourteen Deutschmarks.

Martin sat himself down on the corner of the bed, removed his shoes and slid his feet into the flat white slippers provided by the hotel. The contemporary print on the wall directly in front of him was, he suddenly realised, of an earlier Potsdamer Platz: a central clocktower, a series of intersecting tramlines. The streets, however, were empty. All life had disappeared.

The young architect raised himself from the bed and approached the print. He stared at the artist's signature but was unable to decipher it. All he could glean was that this particular print was number forty-three out of a run of one hundred.

He returned to the bed, laid his head down on the pillow and immediately fell into a deep sleep, waking abruptly some two hours later. He lay there a few moments with his eyes closed, then brought his wrist close to his face. He looked at his watch: it was just after eleven.

Martin walked somewhat unsteadily to the bathroom where he splashed his face with cupped handfuls of cold water. His rejuvenated mind sped back to the events of that afternoon. The opportunity he felt he had squandered would now be given back to him, and manyfold; his time in this city had been blessed.

He turned from the mirror and made his way back to the telephone.

It was his daughter who answered – a brief 'Hello?' followed by a succession of amplified shufflings and abrasions as she adjusted the receiver in her hand. In the background he could hear Sara's voice: 'Who is it, love?' and Naomi's simple answer: 'I don't know.'

Then suddenly her child-voice was booming down the line. 'Who is it?'

'It's Daddy,' he replied.

'It's Daddy,' he heard her yell across the room, and waited in his exhilaration, with the news of his recent meeting and Von Ruhland's offer, listening as the footsteps of his wife approached the phone.

5 Two days later, when Martin arrived, rather breathlessly, suitcase in hand, at Von Ruhland's front door, he was met not by the architect but by a woman in her early twenties, pale, dark-haired, taller by some inches than himself. Having shown him in and called down the long passageway to Von Ruhland, she excused herself and hastened to some distant quarter of the apartment. Von Ruhland made no immediate mention of her, merely greeting the young architect with the results of the election.

'Andrew, hello! It appears we have a new chancellor – Herr Schröder, the first postwar leader too young to remember the Hitler regime.'

Several hours later, Martin was seated in the living room, its central rug rolled back, its furniture pushed against the walls, watching that same young woman, whom he now knew as Anke, pressed close to Von Ruhland, moving rhythmically to a cabaret song of the thirties.

The German lyrics washed over him:

Eine kleine Sehnsucht braucht jeder zum
   Glücklichsein!
Eine kleine Sehnsucht, ein Stückchen
   Sonnenschein.
Eine Sehnsucht für den grauen Tag . . .

He stared at Von Ruhland, at the face and body of a man seemingly decades younger, a body still possessed of immense strength. The body of a father to the child.

The older architect spoke across Anke's shoulder.

'Andrew, enough of this sitting! You must do as I have seen in American films. You must walk up to me, tap me on the shoulder and say, "May I cut in?"'

'I can't dance a step, I'm afraid.'

The two interlocked bodies spun to reveal Anke's face.

'Then I must teach you, *ja*?' she said.

'*Ja*,' said Martin, feeling the word, its breath moving from his mouth.

'Your work,' Martin was clarifying. 'Is it true that none actually remains? Realised work, I mean.'

Anke had long since gone, breaking from Von Ruhland at the end of a song, moving backwards from the room not unlike a courtier, leaving the two architects to talk.

Von Ruhland shifted slightly in the chair – a settling in.

'You know of my history?' he eventually asked.

'A little.'

A wry grin passed over Von Ruhland's face.

'I understand your reticence. You know for instance

about the teenager, privately cited by none less than Tessenow – you will no doubt be aware of that particular reference – the "precocious" teenager recruited from the Technische Hochschule to one of the design teams commissioned to work on the construction of new cities in the occupied territories?'

Martin nodded. Much of this was common knowledge.

'To answer your question: a small number of projects, modified of course by the tyranny of consensus, were commenced. Fortunately, none survived the subsequent bombing. Others never found their way off the drawing board.

'As the course of the war changed, such things as design became an extravagance. Although I believe it is true that even in the last weeks of the war the Führer could be found pondering over plans of cities which had long since been bombed to rubble. Our team was disbanded and the members allocated to positions fulfilling more immediate needs. For reasons never made clear to me I was spared any direct military involvement.

'Afterwards – after the war, I mean – because I was not seen as particularly powerful, any power I had was taken from me. Others from this time, as you no doubt know, have prospered.'

He paused, adding as a type of footnote, 'I feel one needs to adequately pay for the crimes of the past. This judgment was never fully brought upon our nation. Perhaps, in Russia, America found another enemy too soon? That is part of our present problem. We are obliged to negotiate a path between not repeating the past and being obsessed with guilt.'

Von Ruhland shifted once more, slightly, in his chair.

'So there, in a nutshell, you have it. I have continued to live here – it was, as you can readily observe, part of my inheritance – here, and more recently in Potsdam, once the Russians finally relinquished their hold on the family home. What more can I say? For the past fifty years I have been judged – deified or dismissed – on speculation.'

'You never married?' Martin asked.

'No. I have continued to work in private, developing and refining various projects, some of considerable scale. Money, of course, has never been a problem. My father was – how shall I put it? – a minor industrial baron.'

Von Ruhland glanced back towards the mantelpiece clock.

'It is late,' he said. 'And I have a busy day tomorrow. Unless you are an abnormally early riser you shall find me gone.'

The two men stood.

Von Ruhland stepped towards Martin and embraced him, pressing him close – the power of the body astonishing the young architect – then moved him away, hands on Martin's upper arms.

'I appreciate your time here and your company. You know this,' he said. 'There have been many lonely years.'

'Yes,' Martin offered. And such was the poignancy of the moment that he felt the older man might even move to kiss him – an intimate kiss – the thought of which, surprisingly, filled him with no distaste.

'*Träum' gut!*' said Von Ruhland.

Martin woke at three o'clock in the morning with the realisation that he had failed to ring Sara the previous day. It would have to wait some time now – to use his host's telephone at such an hour would be unthinkable.

He lay there in bed, unable to get back to sleep. The events of the previous evening consumed him, in particular his parting from Von Ruhland. What was it that had made him think the older man would kiss him if not his own desire that he be kissed? And would he not have accepted such a thing gladly, this benediction from his master?

His attention was drawn to voices, distant, subdued. Von Ruhland was talking with Anke. He struggled to catch a phrase. He slipped from the bed and walked to the door. They spoke in lowered tones, almost reverent, and – of course! – in German.

6

When Martin rose shortly after ten o'clock the apartment was totally still. He put on the thick brown and blue dressing gown provided by his host and ventured into the hallway. The doors to Von Ruhland's bedroom and study were ajar, but there was no trace of the architect himself. He walked down to the kitchen, a long and rather narrow room dominated by a decorative coal oven at the far end. This cumbersome object was covered in highly glazed blue-green tiles emblazoned with a floral pattern, a tangerine-coloured four-petalled flower; the grim metal door was pale green. On the wall to his right a more contemporary stove had been installed. Next to this on a marble-topped bench were a percolator, a grinder and a jar of coffee beans, presumably left there to attract his attention.

He would make a coffee then ring Sara. He began to calculate the difference in time. In an hour it would be around eight in the evening. Darkness would be well upon the east coast. Both she and Naomi would have eaten their respective meals.

As Martin tipped the beans into the grinder, he heard the front door of the apartment open. Moments later, Anke entered the kitchen carefully carrying a small box surrounded by a plain white paper bag.

'I've bought some things to eat,' she announced, slipping off the paper and levering open the box. 'We have some *Mokkatorte*! And this,' she said, pointing to a cheesecake with cherries, 'is *Quarkkirschkuchen*.'

'They look wonderful,' said Martin. 'And they sound even better. By the way, good morning.'

'*Guten Morgen*,' she replied. 'I see you are thinking of making coffee.'

Martin stared down at his hands still holding the jar of coffee beans.

'I'm sorry. My body's here but my brain is still back in bed.'

Anke took the jar from Martin's hands, placing it on the bench.

'And how was your evening with Johannes?' she asked, flicking the switch of the coffee grinder.

'Very informative,' he replied, raising his voice above the sudden noise.

'So what did you talk about? And don't tell me architecture.'

'History,' he said, after thinking a brief moment. 'We talked about history.'

Anke moved past Martin, carrying the percolator to the sink.

'People who come here who have known places like Paris or Prag say Berlin has no sense of history. But I say its history is in the spaces *between* buildings.'

She tipped the ground coffee into the percolator's small metal sieve.

'You like Berlin?' Martin asked.

'Now it is good. It is the difference between reading about issues and living them. They talk about Berlin having no identity – I think its identity lies in change itself.'

Anke moved to the stove and lit the gas beneath the percolator.

'So we will have our coffee and cake and then you must get yourself ready.'

'Sorry?' Martin managed, somewhat confused.

'Your dancing lesson. Don't tell me you've forgotten?'

The living room had been left as it was the previous evening, the large rug rolled back, the furniture against the walls.

'Now, you are to promise me, you do not panic! Everyone who hears the word "tango" breaks out in a sweat.'

'I promise.'

'And you must be relaxed. You look like a post.'

'Sorry.'

'You cannot be like a post and do the tango. Do you realise women's corsets were changed to woven elastic so they could dance the tango?'

Martin took a deep breath.

'Okay, I'm relaxed.'

Anke moved back from the young architect and looked him up and down.

'I am. I promise.'

She slowly shook her head.

'First we have some fundamentals. When you are moving forward, you keep your feet in a straight line. Don't try and avoid my feet. It's the same when we go backwards. Imagine a line and you are walking on it.

'Don't look down! It ruins your balance and the floor won't tell you anything. Head up so you are looking straight over my right shoulder. I hold you like this,' and she took his right hand with her left. 'Now bend your arm, here, hold it about level with your ear and away from your body. Yes, but curved inwards a little more. Yes.

'Now your left hand should rest lightly on my right

upper arm. For the tango, a little higher and more round the back, so. Keep your fingers neatly together. You are panicking.'

'Sorry.'

'We are going to practise first of all the walk forward. When I say so, you just take a natural step, on the heel first, then the whole foot.'

'God, I must look like a fool.'

'You have my word, no-one is watching you. I will put on some tango music and we will walk together. Don't move.'

Anke released her grip on Martin's hand and went to the record player, leaving him there, arms outstretched like a mannequin. A record had already been placed on the turntable. Anke lowered the stylus onto the first track, then ran back to Martin to re-establish their positions.

'By the end of this afternoon, I promise, you will know the fundamentals.'

7

'Enough!' Martin called.

'You are terribly unfit,' said Anke, moving to the record player and pressing the reject switch.

Martin hobbled to a chair which had been pushed up against a corner cabinet. Anke came and sat on the floor at his feet.

'I'm very glad I'm not wearing an old-fashioned corset,' he said, breathing deeply, looking down at this young woman.

'So, tell me something about yourself,' he asked, after his heart had slowed.

'What would you like to know?'

Perhaps the recent proximity of their bodies seemed to allow Martin more licence in his questions.

'Am I right in assuming you are Johannes' lover?'

'What made you think that?' she said, almost embarrassed.

Martin rushed in with an apology.

'I'm sorry. That was terribly crude, I'm afraid.'

'Johannes has been a father to me.'

'Of course,' he said quickly, then added, 'but he *isn't* your father.'

Anke did not move straight into her explanation, instead waiting a moment, making of it more of a story.

'I was born in the former East Berlin. I was taken from my parents when I was five – they were judged to be politically unreliable, so I was given to an acceptable family.'

'I really am sorry,' Martin said. 'I had no idea.'

'That's all right. I don't mind talking about it.'

'Are your real parents still alive? Do you see them at all now?'

'I have never been able to find out what happened to them. I suppose they were interrogated by the Stasi and sent to prison or the psychiatric clinics, like they had in Russia. In those days people disappeared.'

'Yes,' Martin offered.

'So I was brought up by this other family. One year it

was discovered I had talent and I was sent to one of the sports schools. I was to become a gymnast – my successes would be a valuable contribution to "strengthening our Workers' and Peasants' State and to its international reputation". Then, when I was twelve, I began growing too much. I was suddenly too tall and the school abandoned me.

'The day the Wall came down I walked into West Berlin. I was just fifteen. I found myself staring at this man in his sixties. No, I know that now – when I saw him he was just an older man to whom age did not matter. "Welcome to a new life," he said. We embraced as everyone was doing, stranger holding stranger. After that he invited me to a café. He asked me my story and offered to give me a home. Johannes had no children – I suppose I became a child for him. He looked after me and paid for me to study dance, and eventually I was fortunate enough to join a small company.

'Our last performance was at KulturBrauerei – the old brewery in Knaackstrasse. It was used by the Stasi for many years.' Anke gave a small laugh. 'So I end up dancing above the place where my parents could have been tortured.'

Martin entered his bedroom and moved straight to the large lamp on his desk. It was a dull afternoon and what light there was seemed to have been leached from the air by the dark-timbered furnishings. His suitcase, the single modern object in this room, lay on the floor at the foot of the bed still largely unpacked.

He walked to the window and pulled aside the heavy lace curtains. Below was the building's communal courtyard, much of it obscured by the yellowing foliage of a tree. He could make out what appeared to be a tricycle abandoned on a brick path. He released the lace from his hand, fogging the view, and turned back to the room.

8

Von Ruhland returned late that afternoon.

'I hope you have no particular plans for this evening?' he called to Martin from his study.

'Hardly!' he called back.

'This is good,' said Von Ruhland, now standing in the doorway of Martin's bedroom. 'For some time now I have been negotiating the purchase of a Christian Schad from an art dealer in Hamburg. He handed this on to me.'

Von Ruhland passed the young architect a card. 'We are cordially invited to attend the opening of the exhibition *Berlin/Berlin* at eight p.m. in the Postfuhramt, or words to that effect.'

Martin looked down at the invitation. The front showed an angled view of what appeared to be a late-eighteenth-century building constructed in neoclassical style, the near wing of which was partly concealed behind a temporary wooden fence and draped in sheets of plastic.

'What's the building?' he asked, indicating the card.

'It's the Brandenburg Gate taken from a rather unflattering angle. In the top left-hand corner of the photograph you can see the raised hoof of one of the horses pulling

Viktoria's chariot. You have not visited our humble Arch of Peace?'

'Sadly, no.'

'Then we shall rectify this as soon as possible – tomorrow we shall become tourists!'

Martin turned the card to find Von Ruhland's 'cordial' invitation written in both English and German.

'"This invitation is valid for two,"' he read, and tried the German out loud. '"*Diese Einladung gilt für zwei Personen.*" What about Anke?' he suddenly added.

'Today is a Tuesday – she will be involved in rehearsals. Besides, I'm not convinced Anke has a great deal of time for "modern" art. You are agreeable to going?'

'Absolutely.'

'It is part of the first Berlin Biennale,' he said. 'I make no promises. And afterwards we shall find somewhere to eat nearby?'

The steps leading up to the old Berlin post office were aswarm – a dark-coated mass of bodies slowly funnelling themselves through a single open door.

Martin edged upwards alongside Von Ruhland, his eyes glancing to his feet every few seconds, anxious for a glimpse of an upcoming step. Bodies pressed against him on every side, sometimes assertive, other times teetering, supported by no more than the ascending mass behind them.

Inside proved to be little better. Negotiating the complex spaces required a constant series of manoeuvres and sidesteps. The slightly raised wooden platforms which had been laid down along the corridors on account of the broken-tiled floor beneath only added to the hazardous journey through the building. The architects made their way incrementally from room to room, abandoning some immediately on seeing the thick cargo of bodies inside.

Many of the exhibits showed an almost futurist fascination with movement and speed. Videotapes played with the notion of forwardness and backwardness: a gondola hurtling through a canal; a colour photograph many metres long of a train at a platform, its form variously compressed or stretched. In a large domed space a monstrous industrial fan, suspended from the roof, cut threatening arcs, forcing the stream of spectators to cling to the edges of the room.

'Are you finding this rush hour as intolerable as I am?' Von Ruhland shouted to Martin above the din.

'Intolerably intolerable!' Martin bellowed back.

The two men stopped in their tracks, turned and began the slow passage back against the current of the crowd.

At last they burst their way through the outermost wall of people. Once free, they found themselves laughing, their bodies suddenly loose-limbed. They were schoolboys fleeing from a recent prank. They had left the fussy and futile world of high art behind them. They had reinvented themselves as rebels. They had thumbed their noses at another establishment. It had made them drunk. They stumbled, arm in arm, away from the Postfuhramt.

'Now, the question of where to eat close by, reasonably,

at such a time.' Von Ruhland's enquiry brought them to a sudden halt. 'You have no objection to Italian food?'

'I adore Italian food.'

'Then, my dear Andrew, the answer is simple – we shall go to Café Orange.'

Relinking their arms, they began their journey along Oranienburger Strasse. There was a faint mist in the air, the streetlamps each with a yellowed aura of light. Towards them along the kerbside, slow-moving like an exotic caravan, came a trail of prostitutes, their bodies swaying as if with some arcane affliction brought on by an excess of portrayed desire.

One of the women broke from this parade and approached the two men. She uttered a short phrase in German, then tilted her head to the side and pouted her lips. At Von Ruhland's reply – a hand held against her approach, a simple, *'Nein, danke!'* – the look died instantly. The two men edged past her.

'Schwul,' Martin heard her mutter under her breath as they passed. He did not bother to enquire of Von Ruhland what this word, delivered so derisively, meant. He simply walked on with his companion, past the New Synagogue with its solitary policeman, towards the restaurant.

On his return to the apartment Martin telephoned Sara. He listened to the constant ringing, imagining the space around it and a figure hurrying towards its insistence who would speak with Sara's voice, offering the pleasures of her perfectly ordinary day. But there was no reply. Nor did the answering machine cut in. The phone merely rang itself out.

9

The two architects stood together and moved away from the outside table at Café Einstein, their late-morning coffee spoiled by wasps.

'It seems they are with us a little later this year,' Von Ruhland noted. 'Overstaying the welcome they never had.'

Martin turned back to watch their persistent, belligerent flight, the noisesome creatures laying claim to this space of spilled sugar and cake crumbs.

'Still, we shouldn't complain, weather like this will soon become a distant memory.'

Martin quickened his pace to catch up with Von Ruhland and they continued, side by side, for fifty metres or so before crossing the roadway to walk on the gravel-and-sand median strip of Unter den Linden.

Martin felt a sudden urge to link arms with Von Ruhland as they had the previous night. How else could he hope to indicate the depth of his feelings for this older man? How else signal his appreciation of this time in Berlin? What good a thankyou? He had already said that – to say it again would add nothing.

'If you look up ahead,' Von Ruhland said, breaking Martin's train of thought, 'you will see our destination.'

'So there, courtesy of Carl Gotthard Langhans, you have it, complete with chariot and horses – begun in 1788 and finished some three years later. Our own entrance to the Acropolis, *sans* Acropolis.'

Von Ruhland moved on, so much the guide, walking beneath one of the sets of columns, stopping at the kerbside of the *Platz* before them.

'Out there,' he said, pointing to the centre of a roadway heavy with passing traffic, 'is where the Wall used to be. They have marked it.' And he directed Martin's attention to a double row of rounded reddish bricks set into the surface of the road. The lights changed and the two men crossed the *Platz*.

On reaching the other side, Von Ruhland turned and once more faced the Gate.

'Most people associate this monument with the coming down of the Wall. As for me, I think of a record cover of Dave Brubeck, the jazz pianist. I assume you know of him, even though he was before your time?'

'The "Take Five" man,' Martin said.

'Yes. The Take Five man. I had a long-playing record performed by the Take Five man called *Brandenburg Gate Revisited*. He appears on the front cover standing roughly where we are now, only facing this way, to the camera. Behind him there is the warning about leaving the British sector. I think he is wearing a Russian astrakhan hat, but that would clearly be preposterous. I still have the record somewhere, I shall check. The quartet plays with an orchestra. I haven't listened to the thing for years. I doubt it will have aged well, but one never knows.

'When the Wall was going up, a radio station played

a recording of his "Brandenburg Gate" – it became an instant anthem. Brubeck gave a concert in West Berlin shortly after, and when he began to play the song the audience stood as one.' Von Ruhland glanced down at the line of red bricks. 'Now the Wall has come down I fear they are looking to the buildings to reconnect all the severed threads of the past.'

He looked at his watch.

'It is time to move on. That is the Hotel Adlon,' he said, pointing to his right as they walked back beneath the stone columns. 'For years it was a bombed ruin. Now it is restored to its days of glory. Chaplin stayed there, you may know. And Garbo. Not to mention the good Doctor Einstein.'

Martin stood beside the telephone, his head slightly bowed.

'I'm sorry,' he was saying, 'There've been so many things happening. I rang yesterday but the machine wasn't on.'

'When did you ring?' Sara asked.

'About one o'clock last night, around ten in the morning for you.'

'I'm not sure where I was,' she offered after a short pause.

'It's not important. How's Naomi? Is everything okay?'

'I was picking up the proofs for the Santry retrospective,' she suddenly announced. 'I got back about eleven.'

'That's fine. I thought something like that must've happened.'

'So everything is going well where you are?'

'In Berlin?'

'In Berlin, yes.'

'Yes.'

It ground itself to this momentary halt – the space between their bodies had defeated them. When the silence was broken, they broke it together with their never-to-be-finished sentences, his: 'Sara, I'm sorry about . . .' Hers: 'I'm sorry, I've just . . .'

'You go ahead,' Martin managed to get in.

'I've been missing you, that's all. I'm sorry. When you didn't ring . . .' And she stopped again.

'I'll be home soon.'

'Yes,' she said. 'And here I am spoiling everything for you. Have a great time, Andrew.'

10 The end of the week found the three – the two architects, the dancer – seated around a mahogany table in the dining room.

'I suggest you enlist Anke's help,' said Von Ruhland, tearing a pastry. 'I rarely have the occasion to purchase a gift for a woman. I should inevitably choose the wrong thing: a whisky, a duck-headed walking stick . . .'

'You wish something intimate?' Anke asked.

Martin nodded. He had determined he should make amends for what he felt to be his negligence of Sara. He would purchase a gift of unquestionable value, and the timetable demanded that it be bought today.

'Perfume would be acceptable, if you were coming home from Paris. From Berlin, I would bring home lingerie – what could be more intimate than this? You know her size?'

'She's a twelve,' he ventured.

'We will need to convert that to a German size.' She paused a moment, recalling names. 'There's Hellman. And Kramberg. They are very close. But specifically for lingerie . . .' And then it came to her. 'You are happy to spend a lot of money?'

Martin nodded.

'I think we go to Les Dessous. Or for something younger, more fetishy – is that a word? – there is 'U', just in Fasanen Passage, very close to us. Would you like me to come? I think for you the task may prove difficult and not productive.'

'A perfectly accurate summary,' said Martin. 'I also need to find somewhere that sells toys, for my daughter.'

'For toys, you go to Heidi's Spielzeugladen, near Savignyplatz Station,' said Von Ruhland, looking up from his newspaper.

'How old is your daughter?' Anke enquired.

'Four.' And Martin had a sudden memory of her as he had last seen her, the morning of his departure, loitering near his suitcase, officiating over the final packing.

'Her name's Naomi,' he added.

The two assistants in 'U', one fair-haired, the other dark, were of Anke's age.

'*Guten Tag, womit kann ich Ihnen behilflich sein?*' asked the dark-haired girl, looking up from the counter where she was adding various sums on a calculator.

'*Danke, wir wollen uns nur umschauen,*' Anke replied.

'What was that?' Martin asked.

'I said we were just looking.'

The boutique had about it the 'fetishy' feel of which she had spoken. Almost the entire centre of the floor was taken up by mannequins arranged in staggered formation scarcely two body widths apart – pale emaciated skittles bound in corsets or fine lace. Martin drifted through these figures, none of whom challenged him with their gaze, rather offering their bodies for observation. He stared at each garment, trying to imagine how Sara might appear wearing it. Nothing was suitable; everything was suitable. He felt a small wave of despair flood over him.

He stopped in front of a narrow-waisted *guêpière*, turning to speak to Anke, but she was no longer at his side. He stood on tiptoe, trying to see her amongst the maze of frozen bodies.

He felt the eyes of the two assistants on him.

'What do you think?'

Anke's voice came suddenly from behind him. He turned to find her leaning in a passageway which led to the dressing rooms.

'She will look good like this, *ja*?'

She walked out into the display area modelling a teddy

in flesh-toned crêpe de Chine, taking a path past the two assistants, then threading her way amongst the mannequins, walking the length of the shop.

'*Man könnte Sie für ein Model halten,*' said the dark-haired girl as Anke returned.

'*Und meinen Freund erst recht,*' she replied, moving to Martin and placing her arm languorously across his shoulders.

'Would you like to try something on while you are here?' the fair-haired girl asked him in English.

Martin had no idea what to say.

'I think you would look very becoming in this,' the girl said, coming from behind the counter and holding a pink and black bustier against his chest.

Martin found himself laughing at the absurdity of it all.

'I don't think I have the figure for it.'

'Perhaps then a looser slip?'

He wondered how long he should play this game.

'Not today, thank you,' he said, immediately feeling over-serious. 'I'll just take the one that Anke was wearing. Do you have it in a seventy-five – that's right, isn't it?' he asked, turning to Anke for confirmation. But she had once again disappeared from view.

'Did you see where she went?' he asked the fair-haired assistant.

'I think she went back to the changing rooms.'

'I see. Yes, I'm sure of it. Size seventy-five. And bigger here,' he added, cupping his hands at his chest.

'This is for your wife, is it?' she asked.

'Yes,' he replied. 'It's for my wife.'

The girl left the counter and walked to the opposite wall, which was stocked with garments laid out on wooden shelving.

Martin followed her across the room, picking his way through the mannequins. He found himself in line with the passageway in which Anke had previously appeared. There, halfway down, he saw her, locked mouth to mouth with the dark-haired girl; the teddy had been slipped from her shoulders and was scarcely held in thin folds at her hips.

11

Martin and Anke walked together from the arcade back into the pale, leaf-filtered light of Fasanenstrasse. For a while they remained in silence, as if there were some subject of which they daren't speak. Martin felt the slightest weight of the lingerie bag against his fingers. His time in Berlin was rapidly drawing to a close; the dream of one city would all too soon fade into the reality of another.

The two took a late lunch at the Wintergarten, the secluded café in the grounds of the Literaturhaus.

'You are going Saturday morning?' Anke asked.

'Yes.'

'It's just that I leave myself early this evening. The dance company I am with is performing in Frankfurt on the weekend.'

She gazed sightlessly at the menu, then continued.

'I have enjoyed seeing you here in Berlin. Johannes, you know, he will miss you terribly. You have no idea how important you are to him.' She smiled wistfully. 'Now I am going, you will have the night to yourselves – that will be good.'

'Yes,' Martin replied, echoing her words. 'That will be good.'

A waiter approached their table; Anke spoke briefly to him in German. Martin waited until the young man had moved some distance away before speaking again.

'Is it possible to love two people?' he asked, looking directly at Anke. 'We are taught that love is only possible with one person – real love, I mean. You can't love two people with the same kind of "real love".'

'I fall in love very easily,' said Anke. 'It's a privilege of the young. For example, at the moment I am in love with four different people.'

By way of a pause she followed the progress of a bird's flight between two trees in the garden.

'You have someone who loves you, I assume. You are loved?' she asked.

'Yes.'

'Okay. How many people are you? I mean, are you the same all the time? Isn't there Andrew the architect and Andrew the coffee maker and Andrew the connoisseur of fine lingerie . . .?'

'I suppose so,' he replied.

'Then it's possible. Already someone has loved, or

loves, all the people that you are.' Anke looked Martin directly in the eye. 'But then maybe one can only hold this opinion here, in a city that is accustomed to division.'

They were on their way to the toy shop at Savignyplatz, about to turn right from Ku'damm into Knesebeckstrasse, when Martin came to a sudden halt.

'What is it?' Anke enquired.

'The puppets,' he said. 'Look at the puppets. They're perfect.'

He stood gazing into the window of an antique shop, at a set of hand puppets, each head bearing two faces – Hansel and the witch, Gretel and the woodcutter.

'It's Naomi's favourite story. I tell it to her all the time. She'll love them.' And like a child he knelt down, his head close to the glass. He stared at their faces, the fine web crack of porcelain.

'Do they have a price?' asked Anke.

'No.'

'That is dangerous.'

'I'm buying them no matter what.'

Anke smiled. 'She is a lucky girl.'

'I think I'm the lucky one – it's the perfect gift.'

He stood upright.

'Now I hope to Heaven the shop takes AmEx.'

'In this area if they do not show the price,' Anke said, 'I am certain AmEx will not be a problem.'

12

For those who journey far from home and must return, there is always a last night, a bridging time in which one sorrowfully belongs to neither of the two places. So it was that as Martin's stay approached its conclusion he felt himself increasingly a vagabond, a wanderer without home, and subsequently bound by no jurisdiction.

He had chosen the time after their final meal together to present Von Ruhland with a gift by way of thanks for his hospitality.

The older architect carefully unwrapped a single-malt whisky with a small card attached reading: 'I was unable to find the duck-headed walking stick.'

'This was really quite unnecessary – I feel I should be the one thanking you for spending all this time with me.'

'I think you should also have this,' Martin said, producing from his jacket pocket a small light package which he handed to Von Ruhland.

He weighed the article in his palm.

'No, I have no idea what this might be,' he conceded and began the unwrapping.

'For the smoking room,' said Martin as Von Ruhland lifted the final fold of paper, revealing a packet of American cigarettes.

'You know, tonight might just be the perfect time to surrender to that longstanding temptation. Would you like to join me, Andrew, in taking a cigarette?'

'So, the harbourfront proposal will be foremost in your mind when you return,' Von Ruhland commented.

'That, and another project I've been deliberately avoiding.'

'Through displeasure?'

'Through guilt,' Martin admitted, and went on to explain. 'I've been invited to submit for a competition to design a residential–arts complex in Kyoto, with galleries, performance spaces, and so forth. That was back in July and I haven't had the chance to visit the site yet, let alone develop any concept. I have a feeling I'll be returning the preparation fee with a very apologetic letter.'

'What fee are they offering?' Von Ruhland leant across the arm of his chair, lifting his cigarette from the ashtray.

'Sixty thousand American.'

'They are envisaging a substantial building then.'

In most ways the smoking room was a further extension of the apartment's overall aesthetic – walls papered in an overly ornate design, period furniture, windows drenched in elaborate dressings. Except that various objects – curled hunting horns, riding crops, antlers – declared it to be a domain for men alone.

'I would be interested in seeing the documentation,' said Von Ruhland.

'At one stage I was considering bringing it with me, but then I convinced myself there wouldn't be much free time for thinking.'

'What district are they building in?'

Martin hesitated a moment, bringing the Japanese name to mind.

'Kiyamachi?' he ventured. 'I think that's it.'

'Yes, Kiyamachi. I know it quite well. It's one of the few remaining geisha districts. There's a small river running through it – not that you'd really call it a river so much as a canal, the Takase. Ogai Mori wrote a story about it. Do you know his work?'

Martin shook his head.

'He was a Japanese writer and physician – late nineteenth, early twentieth century. He spent some time in Germany studying medical hygiene. In fact his Berlin apartment has been turned into a museum. He made the first translation of Goethe's *Faust* into Japanese.' Von Ruhland pressed the end of his cigarette to the ashtray, rubbing it back and forth until only dead ash remained. He looked up. 'We in Berlin, however, chiefly know Herr Ogai as the man whose name adorns one of the Sony Center buildings in Potsdamer Platz, complete with its own website.'

'They want the complex built alongside the Takase.'

'Wonderful!' Von Ruhland announced. He rose from his chair and walked over to Martin. 'The news of your work in waterfronts seems to be spreading fast,' he said, placing his hand on the young architect's shoulder. 'Even with a canal, they seek you!'

They had returned to the living room. But no matter what topic occupied their conversation, nothing could turn Martin's mood from one of sadness. For his part, Von Ruhland remained philosophical about the imminent separation.

'As an architect, you should be no stranger to melancholy,' he said, pouring more wine into Martin's glass. 'Remind me, Andrew, was it Nietzsche who spoke of an architect's sadness at the completion of a project – when he discovers that by building it he has learnt something which he absolutely needed to know to carry the project through?'

'Nietzsche, yes,' Martin confirmed and took a long drink of wine.

Von Ruhland returned to his chair near the room's false fireplace, one which nevertheless was faced with authentic Delft tiles.

'Could we have some music?' Martin enquired.

'But of course. Is there something in particular you would like to hear?'

Martin felt suddenly embarrassed at making his request. He waited for several seconds as if considering various possibilities.

'What was that song you were playing my first night here?'

Von Ruhland thought a moment.

'You were dancing with Anke,' Martin prompted.

'Ah yes, I know it, a song from the 1930s by Friedrich Hollaender. You would like to hear the song again?'

Martin nodded over his glass.

'Please.'

'One moment.' Von Ruhland rose from his chair and left the room.

Martin heard a sudden exclamation coming from down

the hallway and Von Ruhland appeared at the door, a record sleeve in his hand.

'You will be pleased to know I have unearthed the famous *Brandenburg Gate Revisited* by Mr Take Five.' He slowly turned the record over, like a gambler whose fortune depends on a certain card. 'So, there is no Russian hat! My mind has been playing tricks on me.'

Von Ruhland once again left the room, reappearing shortly after with another record. He removed it from the sleeve and placed the black vinyl on the turntable.

Martin heard the stylus break into the last dying chord of the previous track, then the seconds of silence with their slow accumulation of decay – the spit and the crackle like some distant applause.

The song began, a melody at first carried by piano alone, then taken up by strings and accordion. There was for Martin an intoxication which owed nothing to alcohol, but rather some disturbance in the humours, occasioning, perhaps because of the impending loss, a sense of yearning.

'Could we dance?' he asked. 'Anke gave me a lesson. I'm certain to have forgotten most of it, but that hardly matters.'

> *Mein Tag ist grau, dein Tag is grau;*
> *lass uns zusammen gehn!*

So the singer began. Martin and Von Ruhland rose from their chairs and moved to the centre of the room.

A state of yearning, yes. And in that state, that

Sehnsucht, he found himself moving just as Anke had instructed. It was then the realisation came to him that she had taught him everything as if he were a woman. That she had, for whatever reason, groomed him for this very moment. The dance confirmed that he was in this place, at this time, by the exercise of a will and a force far greater than his.

When the song finished and the stylus moved into the following track, a piece quite unsuited to dancing, the two men remained there in each other's arms.

13

Sara knew immediately that the person she met at the airport that Sunday afternoon was profoundly different to the one she had seen depart two weeks before. There was a silence to him, a distractedness. Their longstanding rituals were ignored, or rather seemed never to have been known.

When Martin carried Naomi on his shoulders for the walk to the car, he seemed drained by her slight weight, as if he were bearing a large stone. He was bent by her.

'Did you get some sleep on the flight?' Sara asked.

'Not much.'

But she knew this could not account for the dissimilarity she detected. And it worried her.

They continued in an awkward silence across the roadway, Martin with the debilitating child-weight of his daughter about his neck, and Sara wheeling the trolley on which lay the suitcase.

'I managed to get a reasonable parking spot for once,' she said.

'That's good,' he tried, the words drying up in his mouth as he voiced the blundering reply. 'It's difficult getting something close.'

Upon their return to the apartment, it was Sara who decided that Martin should take himself off to bed for a couple of hours, a suggestion he readily welcomed. His was, after all, an exhaustion beyond the physical, labouring as he was under this new-found state of all but bigamy. At least, he was able to tell himself, there was no question of a decision. There was Sara and there was Johannes – he loved them both.

Martin woke early evening. He lay there with his eyes closed and continued to breathe deeply, mimicking the state of sleep. He felt as though he were being watched, that the room was host to another presence, standing silently at the foot of the bed. He woke again an hour later. He reached out for his watch; it was eight o'clock. He could hear Naomi's voice in the living room below and Sara's, a punctuation to his daughter's sentences.

He sat up. His suitcase stood against the far wall. He tossed back the light doona and walked to the ensuite bathroom. A shower, he knew, would cure him of all these worrisome thoughts. Once his head was clear, everything would slot into place; commonsense would flood back to him, and prevail.

Martin walked down the stairway into the main living

area, his arrival met with excitement from Naomi.

'Come and look, Daddy,' she cried, tugging him towards the centre of the room. She let go of his jumper and ran ahead to grab a sheet of paper. 'Look, Daddy,' she cried, holding it aloft by one corner. 'It's my name.'

'That's fantastic, poppet,' he said. 'Did you write that?'

'I wrote it with that crayon, there,' she said, pointing to a pile of crayons. She waved the paper in the air several times, then brought it back to Sara. 'It says Naomi,' she added.

Martin stood there, his hands behind his back, waiting for her to finish.

'While I was in Berlin I found something special for both of you,' he said. He brought his hands out in front of him, offering a package to his daughter and the 'U' bag to his wife. Sara made no move to open her gift, waiting instead to see what her daughter had received.

'Say thank you,' Sara prompted as Naomi placed the package on the floor and sat down beside it.

'Thank you, Daddy,' she said, tearing at the paper. The antique puppets were revealed. Naomi stared at them as though what lay before her were simply two pieces of wood.

Martin realised how dead they looked, lying there in the shallow grave of paper. He would instantly animate them. He picked one up and fitted it on his fingers. He knelt down beside his daughter, showing her the two different faces.

'See, this side is Hansel and this side is the witch.'

'We don't play that game any more,' she said matter-of-factly.

'I'm sure there're lots of new games you can play with them,' Sara tried, glancing down at Martin and slowly shaking her head.

'And now yours?' he asked.

Martin watched his wife carefully unwrap her present – the discreet bag simply bearing the name 'U', then the outer paper, then the tissue, so that the garment, when she held it there in her hand, seemed to be part of the packaging, the true gift lying somewhere hidden within its frail silk folds.

'It's very feminine,' she said flatly.

Martin was unsure what she meant by this.

'What is it, Mummy?' Naomi asked, staring upwards at the garment in her mother's hands.

'It's called a teddy,' she said.

'That's not a teddy!' Naomi laughed. 'That's not a teddy, Mummy!'

'Don't you like it?' Martin asked.

'Yes, of course. It's just not something I'd imagine you buying me, that's all.' She hesitated a moment. 'I'm sorry, it's lovely and now I'm making it sound like I'm ungrateful.'

'You *don't* like it.'

'What is it, Mummy?' Naomi persisted.

Sara knelt down beside her and quietly suggested it was time for her to go to bed, that she'd be up to see her in a minute. She waited until her daughter had climbed the stairs and wandered across the walkway to her room. Only then did she ask her question.

'Why did you buy something like this, Andrew?'

'I couldn't find a duck-headed walking stick,' he said.

'Sorry?'

'It's a joke. It'd take too long to explain. I'm sad you find it inappropriate.' He heard the trace of anger, of indignancy, in his voice. 'What *should* I have bought you?'

'It's not like you, that's all.'

Sara stood there a while in silence, and then she came out with it.

'When you were away, especially during the time you didn't ring, I had this terrible thought that Natalie was over there with you. I couldn't get it out of my head.'

'I see,' said Martin.

'I was even going to ring where she works to find out if she was gone. I'd made up a character and a voice. I'd rehearsed all these lines.'

'Sara —' Martin began.

'I know it sounds mad.' She paused. 'She wasn't there, was she?'

'No,' said Martin, and he heard his voice sounding unconvincing. Though he spoke the truth, he heard himself speak with the intonation of a liar.

They lay beside each other in bed, the husband, the wife, Martin listening to his own incessant prattle, these wretched words, heaping the inconsequentialities one upon another, occupying the space into which he feared would flood her question.

And then it happened. When he had all but exhausted himself, his words holding at bay what he feared the most, Sara reached out to him, to silence him. She wanted to make love.

Any trace of desire drained from him. He knew it was not possible to continue with Von Ruhland's name a secret.

'Sara,' he said, and she knew immediately his unfaithfulness.

'She *was* there!'

'It's not Natalie,' he said.

'So it was just someone you met.'

Martin heard the tone of bitter accusation. He knew he had to speak this name, as he also knew how much power was bound up in its three syllables.

'Johannes,' he said.

She tilted her head. She hadn't heard, or else she hadn't understood.

'Von Ruhland.'

She lay next to him in utter silence.

'What you have to understand is I haven't stopped loving you,' he continued. 'I love you as much now as at any time in our life together. I know it sounds strange, and probably awful to you at the moment, but I know it *is* possible to love two people.' The arguments that had seemed so compelling in Berlin evaporated before him. What had

Anke said that had been so convincing? He lay there a moment, quite speechless.

'I have to ask,' Sara said, and then gathered herself for it. 'Have you been to bed with him?'

'Yes,' he replied. 'The last night –'

'And you used protection? Or *he* used protection?' Adding quickly before he could utter so much as a sound, 'It's all right, I don't want to know.'

So far she had seemed calm, almost uninterested in his confession. This, in its own way, served to encourage him and he moved to touch his wife, whom he loved. But Sara flung herself from the bed as if she had been approached by some diseased thing. She stood, her body half crouched, covering itself, against the bedroom wall, her eyes searching for clothing, anything to shield herself from his gaze.

Martin called her name. It was this word, or else him pronouncing it – 'Sara' – which caused her to cry. Or rather, there issued from her mouth a long deep sound that for weeks afterwards would strike him as the reaction one might have expected at the news of his death. For the young architect's wife, perhaps, it was the same thing – a senseless and irreversible loss to which had been added some kind of humiliation. This particular loss had insulted her and undermined her belief in herself.

For his part, Martin had seen his few words tearing everything asunder. He had watched them run rampant through this space; they might, he considered, as well have been living things, barbarians, sparing nothing.

Martin learnt, at that moment, about a power he alone possessed in this regard, and the cost of its abuse. He looked about him. Naomi was at the bedroom door, her small body confused and vulnerable, her demeanor that of a clockwork doll whose mechanism had run down. He had undone too much.

14

In one of the short exchanges between Martin and his wife over the next two days it was decided that he would move from the apartment as soon as possible. He made enquiries of a number of estate agents with whom he was reasonably well acquainted, settling, sight unseen, on an inexpensive and immediately available furnished flat in Prahran.

In all of this Martin lamented the fact that he had been the one to leave the inner-city apartment – but this should not be taken wrongly. *He* should have been the one, he felt, who, making an ordinary passage from the lounge room to the kitchen, would find his attention captured a second by this ornament, or that card inclined upon a mantelpiece, releasing its history. This pain, he knew, should be his; these memories should tear at his heart, not hers, who had done nothing. He had, with a vast inadvertent cruelty, bequeathed all of this to Sara.

As for Naomi, it was his belief that by having entered into this relationship with Von Ruhland he had somehow forfeited the right to see his child, that this must be a cost of the decision he had made. Whatever the sense in this, it was a judgment and a punishment he had brought down upon himself. So with each return to this one-bedroomed flat he suffered a coming home to silence, with no child's welcome, an absence with no child's lighting face.

He called from his office, leaving the new address on the answering machine in case Sara needed to contact him. He said that he would give her the telephone number as soon as it was connected. He ran through the cold information, thankful that he was reciting it to a machine.

It happened, then, that Martin remained torn by these separate griefs and these separate absences. It would come to him – most often late at night, wearied by another day blighted by distraction – the reconstruction of his final night with Von Ruhland. At such times it presented itself to him not as a single act so much as a number of minute slippages: an excess of emotion which had led to an embrace; an embrace which had led to a kiss; a kiss which, when broken, revealed the hands upon the face, the neck.

And so Martin had found nothing surprising or unnatural, nothing to be resisted, in sharing pleasure with this older man whom he loved and who had, after all, been in his thoughts the entirety of his adult life – nor in giving himself, at first in acquiescence and a willing submissiveness and then in abandon.

Nonetheless, mainly as a consequence of his wife's cry, he could not bring himself to contact Von Ruhland. To do so struck him as involving a sort of impropriety, though this word suggests a certain piousness on his part, which was not the case. It should rather be seen as a form of respect paid during a period of mourning.

Several weeks passed by in this manner.

It was, in the scheme of things, a quite trivial event that occasioned Martin to contact Von Ruhland, if not to speak directly with him. One Friday evening he had driven in to Carlton to have an early dinner with Belsey. He had gone straight from work in order to secure a reasonable parking place and consequently found himself with a good ninety minutes to fill. He took a slow coffee at Tiamo, then ambled the few steps along Lygon Street to Readings bookshop. He cast an eye over the piles of remaindered books on the table inside the door, then headed for the compact discs. As he approached, his eye was immediately taken by a copy of *Brandenburg Gate Revisited* face out on the wall display above the new arrivals section. He hooked the cover from the wall, then hunted through the jazz CDs in search of a second copy.

Later that evening, having shed Belsey – who, it became clear, had seen in the 'Von Ruhland affair' the glimmer of a possibility that he might, in the end, be welcomed as a worthy successor in the young architect's affections – Martin sat listening to the Brubeck and penning a short note to accompany it. 'Dear Johannes, Turn over for the hat!'

For indeed, there on the redesigned back cover was a sepia photograph of Dave Brubeck peering into the camera wearing an astrakhan hat.

15

One evening some days later, Martin was visited by Natalie Vlies.

'I rang Alex Jacobs a couple of days ago,' she said. 'He gave me this address. I wasn't sure whether I should come . . . I was worried.'

Martin showed her in.

'I've heard bits and pieces, you know. It didn't seem right to come straight away.' And she took a deep breath. 'It's like after a death, keeping one's distance so the other person can grieve. I'm making it sound all too grand. Forgive me, Andrew, for all this carry-on.'

Martin had known Natalie Vlies for a little under a year. In this time they had worked together closely on a number of projects, her input, he felt, on various urban waterfront developments being a significant factor in his recent visibility. She was first, then, a valued collaborator.

It was during these periods of collaboration, after work or over a hastily taken lunch, that it had become evident Natalie could also provide the emotional support that Jacobs so assiduously avoided and Belsey trivialised. As a consequence of their developing relationship, Martin had found her name often arising in conversation both at work and at home. This *naming* was the source of his wife's concern – the word 'Natalie', she felt, was not a simple reference or acknowledgment, but a form of infidelity.

In Sara's defence it must be said that the landscape designer had always found Martin attractive and was in awe of what she understood to be a most singular vision. They were in many ways well suited. It happened, though, that the architect continued to be in love with his wife. He had been a faithful man.

'Is this separation from Sara a permanent thing?' Natalie was enquiring, seated on a kitchen chair, a refilled glass of wine beside her on the table.

'You know about Johannes?'

'Von Ruhland? I've heard you met him and stayed with him in Berlin.'

'Did you hear I fell in love with him?'

'I heard something to that effect. But then you always were a bit in love with him, weren't you?'

'Yes,' he answered, thankful of finding at last some validity in his Wintergarten conversation with Anke. 'But I only really found that out in Berlin. The thing is, I don't think my feelings are likely to change, and I can hardly expect Sara to wait for me in case they do. Besides,' he added flatly, 'I'm not sure she'd want me back even if they did.'

Martin took a mouthful of wine.

'To answer your question,' he continued, 'as long as Johannes is in my life,' by which he meant his heart, 'I can't see any reconciliation with Sara.'

Natalie hesitated at the edge of her chair. Should she go to him and hold him? Should she let him be? She was clear about what she wanted to do but was uncertain of its appropriateness.

'Have you spoken with him about all of this?' she asked.

'I sent him a note, last Monday, with a gift . . .'

He stopped. And then, as if it were as much as he could do, he rushed out his confession whilst he had voice enough to express it. 'I haven't spoken to him. I haven't told him my number or address.'

'Why?' she asked, knowing the answer as soon as she had spoken.

And Martin, who had managed to control his emotions through the past weeks, alone in his flat or sitting opposite a friend in a café, was suddenly brought to his senses, in the fullness of its meaning – to the longing he felt to be again with the older architect, to the damage he knew this longing had already wrought, to the fear of voicing this desire lest it all be taken from him. His body shuddered for a moment and then seemed to fold in upon itself.

Natalie moved to him, held him.

'Andrew, you have to know where you stand. And so does Johannes. How do you know he isn't worried to death about not hearing?'

She paused a moment as if needing to gather herself. When she spoke again her voice betrayed a certain sorrow.

'You have to find out what the future holds,' she said. 'If there *is* a future. And how to move on.'

In her arms he tried, time and time again, to make the simplest of affirmations, but his breath would not hold and he would gasp for air, the single syllable beyond him. Until it was Natalie who spoke for him, saying, 'Yes.' And Martin, his body trembling with the thing now spoken, found the strength at least to nod out his agreement.

As a result of this time with Natalie, the following evening Martin determined he would ring Von Ruhland. He sat down with a sheet of paper and wrote a list of hours, beginning from the present time, ten o'clock at night. The translation was a simple one – it would be two o'clock in the afternoon. And at eleven in the east of Australia it would be three o'clock in Berlin. The time at which he had first met the older architect. He chose this time.

At five minutes to midnight he was seated by the telephone, the full number with its country code and its city code transcribed onto another sheet of paper resting on his lap. Beside him was a half-filled glass of cabernet.

Just before midnight Martin finished the wine in one draught and dialled. The phone rang with its characteristic tone, one, two, three times. Then he heard Von Ruhland's voice.

'*Hallo?*'

'Hello, Johannes, it's Andrew.' And he heard only silence.

'Andrew Martin, the architect from Australia.'

'Andrew, how are you?'

'I'm okay,' he said, feeling his voice quavering. 'And you?'

'I am well.'

'There's a surprise for you in the mail. I only posted it on Monday.'

'I look forward to receiving it.'

When he had made the decision to ring, Martin had imagined the conversation would proceed as it had in

Berlin, the older architect leading, filling the spaces with fact and opinion. He wasn't in the least prepared for Von Ruhland's simple answers. His brain sped. Already there had been an awkward silence. For the first time it occurred to him that maybe this man placed no importance at all on what had happened over those seven days, over that night, in Berlin. And why should he? What use does a master have for another pupil?

Suddenly Von Ruhland's voice was on the line.

'What have you rung to tell me, Andrew? That you have told your wife about our time together?'

'Yes.'

'And that she saw it differently from you?'

'My marriage . . .' he began, then broke off. 'There's nothing now in that relationship. It's over. I've moved out to a small flat. My work has suffered.'

'So, things are difficult for you, Andrew.'

'I shouldn't have rung. I just wanted –'

'There is no need for you to apologise.' Von Ruhland waited a moment. 'But I wonder, what do you intend to do now?'

Martin did not know how to answer this question. Like Natalie earlier that evening, he knew what he wished – to return to Berlin, that very day if it were possible – but as to what he might admit, he had no idea.

'If you have no better plan,' Von Ruhland continued, 'why not come back to Berlin? You are more than welcome, and for as long as you wish.'

16 Martin was unprepared for that early November weather. The wind was bitter, carrying with it a taste of salt. He shivered in his black three-quarter coat, not buttoning it but folding it about himself like a blanket.

He watched the taxi drive off down Fasanenstrasse, leaving him standing alone with his suitcase.

'What is this you are wearing?' Von Ruhland laughed as soon as he opened the apartment door. 'You may as well be dressed in an Hawaiian shirt!'

He stepped aside to let the younger man enter, taking the suitcase from him as he passed.

'Tomorrow, we shall visit KaDeWe and buy you a coat worthy of a Berlin winter.'

'How was your flight?' Von Ruhland asked, placing the coffee pot on the kitchen stove.

'There is nothing more dismal than arriving at Heathrow around five-thirty in the morning and waiting for a flight all the way back to Berlin.'

'You will get no sympathy from me. You should have flown with Lufthansa.' Von Ruhland took a seat at the kitchen bench.

'Is Anke still living here?' Martin asked.

'Anke, my dear Andrew, has become a veritable star. Do you recall the Frankfurt performance? I think she was heading there the evening before you left?'

Martin remembered that day.

'It went well. And now it seems they have a commission

from somebody or another to tour half the cities in Germany. One moment.'

Von Ruhland left his seat and adjusted the gas on the stove.

'Now, before I forget, I must thank you for the Brubeck, which only just arrived before you. Unfortunately, I do not own the equipment necessary to play such an object, which makes the photograph of Mr Brubeck in his astrakhan hat one of the most oddly framed pieces of art I own.'

'Does this KaDeWe sell electronic equipment?'

'Andrew, KaDeWe is the very symbol of capitalism. It's the second-largest department store in the world – the food hall sells over one thousand varieties of German sausage.'

'Then allow me to introduce you to the joys of the compact disc player – no more scratchy records.'

'But I love the scratches. And the pops, and the crackles – without them the music would have no history.'

After dinner that evening, Martin took from his suitcase the documentation for the Kyoto project and brought it through to the dining room for Von Ruhland to see.

The older architect slowly worked his way through the package of materials.

'"An accommodation complex for visiting painters, musicians, writers,"' he read out loud. 'No architects, mind you, "with accompanying exhibition and performance spaces."' He turned a further page. 'Ah!' he continued. 'They are building it on the site of the old elementary school.'

Von Ruhland turned through several more pages.

'So, you would need to speak to a design in January. You have done some work on this since we last met?'

'Still nothing, I'm afraid. In the scheme of things, it's been rather lost.'

'And the result will be announced when?'

'Early April.'

'But of course,' Von Ruhland said, going on to explain. 'The street that runs alongside the Takase, Kiyamachi-dori, is lined with cherry trees. In April they will be in blossom – the effect is quite breathtaking.'

'What took you to Kyoto?' Martin asked, and brought the after-dinner port to his lips.

'Shadows,' came the reply. 'I had developed an interest in shadows, and buildings which might be seen to manufacture them in various densities. I was in Kyoto taking certain measurements.'

The following day saw a late burst of clear weather.

'You see,' said Von Ruhland. 'As soon as one purchases a coat, the weather responds with a near-perfect afternoon.'

The two men wandered together through the Tiergarten, Martin carrying on his arm the new full-length black coat with its astrakhan collar. In the coat's pocket was folded a matching Russian hat, purchased by Von Ruhland, at his insistence. 'In honour of our dear Mr Brubeck.'

The older architect gestured broadly in front of him.

'This whole area was originally the Great Elector

Friedrich Wilhelm's hunting grounds, with wild boar and deer conveniently fenced in over an area of three square kilometres.' He smiled. 'I like the Tiergarten – it is a perfect English park complete with an angel. The Siegessäule – our beloved Gold Else.' Von Ruhland nodded in the direction of the Victory Column.

'The Nazi regime moved her from Königsplatz, in front of the Reichstag, to here,' he said. 'She would have obstructed the crossing of the two main axes of Germania. The Führer's dream city was supposed to be finished in 1950. About the only part of the plan which is still visible is the row of double streetlamps on Strasse des 17. Juni.' And he pointed back towards his left.

'Did you know Speer?' Martin asked.

'I saw him briefly around the end of 1941, the beginning of 1942, before he became Doctor Todt's successor. He was, as they say, a very charming man – polite, intelligent – but an incurable romantic. Only a romantic could have come up with the proposition that buildings be designed with an eye to their attractiveness as ruins in some distant future.

'There has always been this speculation concerning his relationship with the Führer. To my eyes, Speer was clearly in love. Besotted. As for Hitler, when speaking to the architect, I believe he never once used *du*.'

They continued their slow perambulation through the park, the afternoon sun diagonally hitting their right cheeks. Von Ruhland brought his hand to his face, shielding his eyes from the light.

'I remember the Tiergarten after the war,' he said, almost in a type of trance. 'The winter of 1946–47 was particularly cruel – early all the trees here were chopped down for firewood. I can see it now, an open space bordered by ruins. The place was a vast potato field. I can remember the pickers and their huge sacks.

'Over there is the zoo. Most of the animals were killed in the bombing raids. The last elephant was driven insane by the noise. If I recall correctly, its name was Siam. They say it trumpeted ceaselessly in terror.'

Over dinner that evening Von Ruhland seemed particularly quiet – absorbed, it seemed, by some unspoken issue. As soon as the meal was finished, he pushed back his plate in a definite gesture, as if somewhere deep within him a decision had been made.

'Let me share something with you,' said Von Ruhland, standing at the table's end. 'Something no-one else has seen.'

He motioned Martin to follow him down the passageway to the study. Martin watched their dimly lit reflections approach, speeding towards them, hell-bent on collision.

Von Ruhland pushed open the study door and switched on the overhead light.

'Come,' he called.

Martin stood just inside the door. He had passed by this room on a number of occasions, but this was the first time he had fully seen the space in which Von Ruhland worked. He watched as the older architect approached an ancient mahogany *Planschrank* situated on a windowless wall and pulled out the top drawer.

Von Ruhland withdrew a number of plans and carried them to the work table. He turned on the lamp directly above, illuminating the drawings in a clear white light, then called the young architect to his side.

'Here,' he said, pointing at the first sheet. 'And here,' pulling away one drawing to reveal another. 'And again.'

Martin stared in awe at the breadth of vision.

'How long ago was this done?' he asked as Von Ruhland revealed a plan of what appeared to be contemporary terrace buildings.

'About thirty years ago. Possibly more.'

'Thirty *years*.'

'They were ahead of their time, yes.' Von Ruhland pulled out another sheet. 'Some of my concepts from the fifties are beginning to be acceptable now, as demonstrated in the works of others, of course.'

The vast array continued, Martin asking Von Ruhland to pause every so often as he saw designs in far more sophisticated versions than his own, frightened to ask when they had been drafted, knowing full well how long ago the older architect must have encompassed these particular visions.

'And none of your work has been realised,' Martin said, a frustrated anger arising in him at the waste implicit in this. At the injustice. 'How can you go your whole life without a building being completed?'

'Tell me frankly,' Von Ruhland replied, 'what choice do I have?'

17

The following evening, Martin dined alone at Wellenstein, seated at a table on a blood-red velvet chair. The air was thick with smoke. He stared at the unframed canvasses above the bar, people unknown to him from what appeared to be the 1920s.

Von Ruhland had informed Martin he would be arranging some financial matters in Berne most of the day, and expected to be home by eight.

'But you must not wait for me,' he had said. 'These trips have a habit of taking longer than you think. Get yourself something to eat on Ku'damm. Wellenstein is good and very reasonably priced. I think you'll find it at number 190.'

Martin's gaze drifted upward to the high ceilings, then down the parchment-peach of the painted wallpaper to the red café curtains with their brass rods on the windows near the street.

At a nearby table, two men – one with dark hair and of pale complexion, the other fair-haired with an ill-defined goatee – were conversing in English. He could catch the occasional exchange of dialogue. The dark-haired man spoke with a German accent: 'For example, should one read any significance into the fact that the collapse of the Wall happened on the same day as Kristallnacht?'

'Or on the same day that you decide to invite me out to dinner?'

The waitress brought Martin's meal: a dish of venison served with noodles, a glass of *Rotwein*.

By the time he let himself into the apartment shortly before nine o'clock, Von Ruhland had still not returned. Martin went to the living room and chose one of the five CDs in his host's new collection – a reissue of Klemperer conducting Mahler's Second Symphony. As the violins and violas gathered themselves, trembling, and the lower strings made their swift assaults, he walked through the open doorway into the dining room and from there into the passageway.

Deep in the apartment he glimpsed a man moving from a lighted room. The reflection frightened him, so distant it was barely recognisable as himself. He moved towards it, as it to him. Martin found himself making no sudden movement, lest this darkening vision fail to respond and he would know himself dead in this apartment, no longer a part of this city, or this Earth.

He approached with stealth, his hand slowly rising to the level of the light switch he knew to be two-thirds of the way down the passageway. His fingers found it, slipped across its smooth curved housing.

With the light, the ordinary world flooded in. There was an architect in his early thirties poised a moment in the passageway of a Berlin apartment. Nothing more, nothing less.

Martin reached the end of the passageway, but instead of turning towards the bedrooms, he was drawn to

Von Ruhland's study and, within it, the drawers of the *Planschrank*, for he knew well that the other night he had glimpsed only a fraction of the material contained in its dark embrace. His hands hesitated before the brass handles. Of what was this man capable? He chose the second-last of the eight drawers. It rolled out smoothly.

At first he was unsure of what he saw, until the scale of the drawing became apparent. Before him was the first of what proved to be several plans, each a part of the whole which was a vision for the reconstruction of Berlin. He lifted more of the sheets, finding upon their various papers, older and newer, plans for the reconstruction of other cities. He read the names – London, Moskau, Rom. Page after page adding to the list. Kairo, Venedig . . .

18

Von Ruhland was seated at the dining-room table turning the pages of a magazine.

'There's fresh coffee,' Martin announced, walking in from the kitchen.

'Thank you,' the older architect offered. He tapped a page of the magazine. 'This century has perfected mass murder. And it has done little to enrich our vocabulary with terms to describe and evaluate it. The sheer weight of its anonymity becomes its first line of defence.'

Martin moved round behind Von Ruhland and stared down at the page: a headline, LEBEN IM WALD; a map of Kosovo; a photograph of a pit on the slope of which stood two soldiers, in front of whom a rectangle of plastic sheeting some two by four metres was held in place by large rocks. Below the photograph was a caption, '*Massengrab bei Klecka*', and below that, '*Typisch balkanische Greuelgeschichte*'.

'It wasn't so long ago, seven or so years, that young German neo-Nazis were being trained in Bavaria to kill for the Ustashe, the independent legionnaire corps fighting against the Serbs, but also against the Bosnian Muslims who, ironically enough, had been in the SS during the war.'

Martin stared at the small colour photograph. 'If ever we needed an argument for the non-existence of God, things such as this are surely it.'

Von Ruhland looked up from his magazine.

'And what would *prove* His existence?' he asked. 'Should the true God strike down the guilty? Avenge the innocent? A merciful God would cease to exist as soon as He acted. To avenge the innocent would make Him the greatest murderer ever known. "He who fights with monsters might take care lest he thereby become a monster," as Nietzsche once put it. In this life I expect no punishment from God. My God intervenes only after death, and by that I mean the death of all mankind.'

Martin grew concerned about Von Ruhland. Perhaps it was the breakfast conversation, but the older architect remained morose and taciturn for most of the day. His inner being seemed to be in a state of turmoil. Over their evening meal together, Von Ruhland spoke not a word. It was as much as Martin could do to obtain even a nod, the slightest of acknowledgments.

Then he spoke.

'My dear Andrew,' he said, 'there is something you must know. Something from the past I have to make clear to you. If it would please you to come with me now?'

'Of course,' said Martin, standing quietly and pushing his chair back beneath the table.

Von Ruhland entered the study. On this occasion, though, he walked directly to a cabinet below the room's only window. He reached in his pocket and withdrew a set of keys. Selecting one, he bent down and unlocked the bottom drawer of the cabinet. From inside he carefully removed a set of drawings which he carried to the work table.

'The building tells us little of its purpose. You will notice there are no designated spaces for sexual activity, or for perfect sleep. No space has been provided for pets. There are no smoking rooms.'

The design which Martin looked at was for a construction of immense size. Many of the German terms, particularly in their abbreviated forms, were unknown to him.

'What is *Vorr.*?' he asked.

'Entrance room.'

'And *Schrank u. Ankleidez.*?'

'Dressing room.'

'*Bad u. Ab.*?'

'How would you put it – bathing room?'

Von Ruhland began pointing to other sections of the building. 'And these are the waiting rooms. These are the information rooms, and this the Great Hall.'

Von Ruhland stepped back from the table.

'I have spoken of my precocity,' he continued. 'Some of those within the design team were prepared to speak of me as a visionary. Perhaps they felt it somehow enhanced their own reputations to have acknowledged this, to be amongst the first to name genius when they saw it.'

He ran his fingers over the paper as though verifying its existence.

'The very first experiments with mass gassing took place as early as September 1941. Some months after this I was called into the office of Herr Glaubrecht, one of the senior architects. There was a new commission he had been given. He told me he was placing this wholly in my hands. I was to tell no-one. I was to work on the design of what would now be called an ethnic-cleansing complex, which was to deal with extermination, with systematic genocide, after the defeat of the Allied forces. It was to be on a monumental scale.' The architect looked down upon his drawings.

'Inscribed in these lines as clearly as the path of my own signature is my responsibility.'

Martin stared at the name of the town, Kranzenthal; he looked at the exquisite hand which had made its mark so lovingly across the paper.

'Does it look so different to any other building?' the older architect said.

Martin slowly shook his head – a 'no', or merely the expression of disbelief.

'Like so many others, it was never finished. And the proof that such a thing was even contemplated? Just a long-abandoned railway line finishing at the scars of excavation, some piddling foundation work – barely a gesture.'

Von Ruhland turned to Martin and held him by the shoulders, as he had that first night of his stay. Martin met his eyes.

'Can you still love someone who would design such a thing?' Von Ruhland asked.

Martin paused only for the slightest moment, enough to reassure himself his answer was not simply automatic.

'Yes,' he said.

19

Late one afternoon Von Ruhland emerged from his study, calling for Martin.

'Yes,' he called back. 'I'm in the living room.'

Martin heard the footsteps approaching down the passage and moving through the dining room, heard their fall on board, rug, but with more sense of urgency than he had ever noticed before.

'Andrew,' he announced from the doorway, 'I have some work which craves to be completed. I'm not sure how long this will take – I would guess somewhere between two to three days. But I will need absolute solitude. You must forgive me.'

'I can take a room at a hotel –'

'No, no, no,' Von Ruhland interrupted, 'there is no need for anything so dramatic. It just means that you will have to fend for yourself over this time.'

'That's fine,' Martin replied. 'I can cook your meals –'

The older architect interrupted once again. 'Thank you, but no. I would prefer no disturbance at all. I will need to pull the plug on the telephone, for instance. As long as you are prepared to excuse me for this time, that is all I ask.'

'Most certainly,' said Martin. 'If I weren't here, you'd have the conditions you want. Are you sure you wouldn't prefer me to stay somewhere else?'

'I will hear no more of it,' the older architect announced, and he turned on his heel, hastening into the body of the apartment.

Martin pushed the sleeves of his pullover back to the forearm and took a drink of coffee. The postcards he had purchased that morning were spread out before him on the dining-room table – a panorama of a city that no longer existed, a Berlin of the twenties and thirties. He gazed down on the black and white images: *Blick zum Brandenburger Tor* – a view along Unter den Linden to the Brandenburg Gate, the young linden trees still supported by stakes, the very path he had taken with Von Ruhland almost seventy years later. *Nachtzauber in Berlin*: on this particular 'magical night' in Potsdamer Platz the hands of the clock tower read seven minutes to two, the darkness riddled with electric signs – 'Haus Vaterland', 'Hotel

Fürstenhof', 'Konzert-Kaffee' – but as in the print on the wall of his room at the Kempinski, the streets of the *Platz* were completely empty.

In his head he began compiling a list of friends and acquaintances to whom he might assign the cards: Jacobs, his business partner; Belsey, his oldest acquaintance, for whom the shot of Dietrich in a sailor's cap became an obvious choice; Natalie Vlies... It was a list which would have once begun with the names of his wife and daughter.

He resolved that the proper thing to do was write a letter to Sara informing her of his return to Berlin and enclosing a cheque to comfortably cover their expenses for the month. He took another mouthful of coffee and reached for his notebook, determined he would draft the letter now.

'Dear Sara,' he began, then sat staring at the lined page. Neither the coldness of 'Enclosed please find a cheque' nor the gestural 'I have returned to Berlin' were appropriate. And how to finish this letter, if indeed it could be begun, caught between the unsuitability of 'love' on one hand and on the other the ironic vulgarity of 'yours'? This was obviously not the right time.

Martin raised the unlit cigarette to his nose and inhaled the tobacco. It was a scent belonging to an adolescence long forgotten. A scent of moments alone, of secrecy and of transgression. He struck the match, drew until he heard the faint crackle, then inhaled – here in the room designated for that very purpose. He rose from his chair and walked to the window opposite, staring down across the courtyard through the contours of the leafless trees. As he looked it began to rain, the drops wind-driven to fine broken threads across the pane. The abandoned tricycle was no longer to be seen.

'Dear Sara . . .' After all, what could now be said? Nothing that could repair the damage. A relationship reduced to matters of business. He began, in this solitude, to realise how lost she was to him; she had gone, taking with her not only their child but all the thoroughly replaceless words and situations, all the fine expressions of her face, and most of all the look that once spoke of her total love – and she would never return. So this was the irreparable situation he had created by blindly following the unexpected clamour of his heart – as if it could have ended any other way than this, with Sara alone, torn from their marriage, stumbling through the hours with her lopsided pain.

20

Martin irritatedly pushed the English literary supplement aside. For as long as the older architect continued to remain sequestered in the study, he felt entirely without focus. The postcards and the necessary letter remained unwritten; any engagement with his own architectural practice struck him as thoroughly unpalatable – Jacobs' emails languished in their growing line at the studio he had leased from Zeichenwerk; the Kyoto project was little more than a distant possibility.

What had been bequeathed to him, he understood, was an uncommon restlessness. During the day he wandered aimlessly about the nearby streets, returning impatiently early afternoon to the apartment, only to pace the furthest rooms. Deep in the night Martin would find himself awakened from a half-sleep by the sound of a cistern or the distant hammering of a kitchen tap – noises which may have come from an apartment below.

Late into the evening of the third day Von Ruhland emerged. At the time Martin was seated in the dining room, the postcard images of Berlin still spread out at the opposite end of the table.

'It's done?' Martin enquired with hopeful anticipation. 'The work's finished?'

In answer Von Ruhland proffered several sheets of loosely rolled drafting paper.

'I would like you to look at these,' he said, spreading out the stiff transparent sheets on the dining-room table.

A detailed design for the Kyoto project was laid there before him. Like all profundities, the central concept was the inconceivable which, when seen, seemed obvious. Once again, looking at the older man's work, Martin felt that these were plans of which he might possibly conceive, but only by positing a future many years from now.

'You did these over the past three days,' Martin said, in an astounded half-statement, half-question.

'You like them?' Von Ruhland asked.

Martin laughed aloud, so absurdly did this question strike him.

'Of course!' he uttered. 'They're astonishing.'

'I based them on my impressions of the site plans and from my own memory of the existing building, which has been quite lovingly incorporated. You see the concept? How the building is frozen at the point of obliterating itself. The melancholy of which we have spoken. Hokusai's *Great Wave*. There will need to be refinements, of course.'

The two men sat together in the living room.

'Not all my recent time in isolation was spent on bringing an idea to fruition. As I was meditating on the possibilities of the building, I found myself also drawn to a conversation we had a week or so ago. You may recall your concern that my life had so far passed by without a project being completed?'

'Certainly.'

'At this point, were I a smoker, I would pause to light a cigarette before pursuing a line which is, how shall I put it, quite delicate.'

Martin waited in silence for him to continue.

'You spoke earlier of your astonishment and I thank you from the depths of my heart for this compliment. But again, what will happen to these "astonishing" plans? Are they simply to be added to the pile of drawings, forever languishing, awaiting some future biographer's praise or condemnation?'

Von Ruhland slowly rose and made his way to the false fireplace.

'I have been thinking of the competition,' he said, leaning on the mantelpiece. 'I of course was not invited to submit – why should I be? – and in any case, who now would be prepared to realise my plans?'

He toyed with a porcelain figurine, a sixteenth-century prince, rolling it in his hand then placing it back on the shelf.

'How can I ask?' he said, almost to himself, then addressed Martin directly.

'Could you find it in your heart, and in your conscience – because what I am going to suggest involves a deep dishonesty – could you be persuaded to submit these plans to the competition, electronically redrafted under your name?'

Martin found himself trembling – a *frisson* – at the idea. Its daring, its illicitness.

'Of course, if you still wish to develop some concept of your own, or merely feel a distaste for such an act, I will withdraw the suggestion and in its place offer my most humble apologies. However, before you answer, before you pass judgment on me for this act of overweening pride, can I say, whatever your decision, that you, my dear Andrew, have given me my life back again.'

Martin felt a rush of fulfilment. He alone in the world had been chosen as this criminal. He savoured the peculiar taste of sin in the pursuit of art, and of justice.

'If it's what you want, of course I'll do it,' he said, barely able to speak the words. 'You know I'd do anything to see your work realised.' He remained silent a moment, fighting to control the tremor in his voice. 'But if this design were to win... could you bear to see it under another's name?'

'That it would exist at all would be an exquisite pleasure; that it would be executed under your name would be some repayment for the energy you have restored to my life.'

'Needless to say, I'll pass the preparation fee on to you –'

'The money is of no concern to me. But rather than it becoming an issue, let us agree to subtract from it your expenses – the trip to Kyoto speaking to the design, the cost of modelling, and so forth – and then merely halve the remainder.'

'And were it to win?'

'Let us deal with this when it happens.'

'But it *will* happen,' Martin said. 'We both know that.'

21

It was after one in the morning when Martin felt satisfied that the task had been completed – the meticulous redrafting and animation of Von Ruhland's design in his own electronic signature. He exited the customised CAD program he had installed on the equipment provided by Zeichenwerk as part of their studio leasing agreement.

He rose from the chair and slowly stretched his body. Although it was late, although this final session had kept him many hours at the keyboard, he was tired, it struck him, from the sheer exhaustion of occupying Von Ruhland's place. It was the exhaustion of an actor engaged in the impersonation of a far greater man. He checked the studio door, let himself out of Zeichenwerk, and began the walk back to Fasanenstrasse.

Martin clicked off the bathroom light and moved down the darkened passageway of the apartment, his dimly lit form suddenly occupying the mirror. That his own face should surprise him with its weariness would have been of little concern, except the registering of that surprise seemed to lag behind, the residue of his prior expression hanging a moment in the silver of the mirror as if momentarily lodged there. He moved further forward, his hand raised slowly to touch that other approaching hand. His courage, he felt, had dispelled any demons he had created within. He started to turn, to head towards the bedroom, when he felt the slightest tug upon his pullover – it had brushed against the old wooden frame and caught. Martin looked down at the inch-long loop of fine wool. Beneath his breath, he cursed.

Within a fortnight Von Ruhland's plans had been submitted to the competition under Martin's name. Once more the two men were united by a sense of conspiracy; once more they were errant schoolboys running arm in arm from the scene of a misdemeanour.

Martin was to travel to Kyoto to speak to the design in January. This journey from Berlin recommended itself as a natural time to continue on to Australia, a time to re-establish his networks and to normalise the operations of the company he shared with Jacobs.

Any sadness Martin felt was ameliorated by a belief that he would shortly return. He remained convinced that he was embarking upon another chapter of his life and that it would be intimately bound up with that of the older architect. The living room's rug would once again be rolled away, the furniture pushed against the walls, the record player would be resurrected to provide its hiss and click of thirties cabaret. As they had those months before, the two architects would dance together to *'Eine kleine Sehnsucht'*.

22

The phrase returned to Martin as he climbed the stairs to the Prahran flat, his body enveloped in forty-degree heat: *kyo no sokobie*, the local saying for that fierce, bone-chilling cold he had recently experienced on the snow-covered streets of Kyoto.

Only a day earlier he had trampled the footpath west along Oike-dori to Karasuma-oike subway station on the way back from his presentation session. Before the judging panel – five councillors and various respected members of the cultural community: a professor of architecture, a woodblock printer, a shakuhachi player, a master of the tea ceremony – he had outlined the philosophy and the dynamics of Von Ruhland's design, its functionality and its aptness to what was seen as the essential femininity of Kyoto.

Martin let himself into the brooding heat of the flat's main room and looked around. The venetian blinds were set as he had left them, curved to direct the overspilling light towards the ceiling. He placed his suitcase next to the coffee table and draped his heavy winter coat across the back of the sofa. He walked to the far end of the blinds and, having adjusted them to a fully open position, reached between the thin metal slats to unlock the window. The fierce northerly wind rushed into the room.

Perhaps now, he considered, the time had come to rid himself of this wretched space. But something told him that to move once more would be a waste of effort, given his unspoken aspiration to eventually spend at least half of every year in Berlin. Until such a time, he could see how these ugly and inhospitable rooms might still serve their purpose as a form of penance.

He brought his suitcase through to the bedroom, swung it on the bed and released the catches. He removed his crushed jacket from the top and carried it over to the built-in wardrobe. Before placing it on a hanger he checked the pockets: a fountain pen, a boarding pass, and the two packets of Hope cigarettes he had purchased from a vending machine at Kyoto Station.

'I'm glad to hear the Japanese inquisition went well,' said Jacobs, glancing back over his shoulder as he poured the coffees.

A cool change had passed through Melbourne the evening before and the office windows were flecked with rain:

fine scratches, like so many marks made by fingernails.

'Not that you can ever be certain,' Martin replied. 'Especially with such unreadable judges. The questions tended to be about costs and technical details – I'm taking that as meaning the design itself left them speechless.'

The two men stood together in the tea area of the large open-plan office, from where Martin could see several workstations: Michael and Felicity, captives to the 3D building quietly rotating on their computer screens; Gregor, his book of regulations and his colour catalogues held upright by a sample brick; and, at the far end of the office, as if the space had been organised along historical lines, the CAD-illiterate Bill Perrins happily sketching out some concepts on one of the few remaining drawing boards. Behind them all, the panoramic backdrop of Melbourne lay clouded by the weather and by the very point of observation, here, some forty storeys above the grid of streets.

'Never been to Kyoto myself,' Jacobs remarked. 'What's it like?'

'Nothing at all like I'd imagined,' Martin admitted, bringing his attention back.

'You take sugar, don't you?' Jacobs interrupted, a spoon poised in his hand.

'Only in espresso.'

'I can never get that right, can I?'

'I always thought it'd be an old city, full of temples, palaces, that sort of thing,' Martin continued. 'Like you were stepping back in time.'

'Well, the pictures you see of it certainly give that impression.'

'Yes, but if the frame were wider you'd likely as not find a bicycle shop on one side of the shrine and a fast-food outlet on the other.'

Jacobs passed one of the coffees to Martin.

'And I have to say the CBD reminded me of Melbourne more than anything else.' He paused, seeking some means of describing how he had felt about the city from the brief glimpse he had seen of it. 'It seems caught between two contradictory desires – to preserve its past and to become a modern city.'

'When's the competition announcement, remind me?'

'In the first week of April.'

'So,' Jacobs said, rubbing his hands together, 'that's it. We just keep our fingers crossed till then.'

Martin took a sip of coffee, looking once more beyond his business partner to the city laid out below. 'What's been happening in the old town while I've been away?'

'You've come back right in the middle of a stoush: Carlton Residents Association versus Melbourne University and the Minister for Planning and Local Government. Can we sit down?'

'Of course.'

'My place or yours?' Jacobs asked, nodding his head to the left.

'Yours'll be fine,' said Martin and the two men carried their coffees past the small reference library to Jacobs' office.

'The university had a $250 million project to build four multi-storey buildings in University Square to house its private university. There was going to be a retail centre and two hundred or so serviced apartments. All that needed to be done was demolish thirty-five buildings, including – and here it starts to get awkward – about eighteen or so terraces classified by the City Council and the National Trust.'

'I see,' said Martin.

'It gets worse,' Jacobs continued. 'The whole project gets fast-tracked by the Minister on Christmas Eve – no public input, no public appeals.'

'So what's the current state of play?'

'The last thing I heard was the National Trust had come up with some alternative plans and drawings which they were showing the vice-chancellor.'

Martin watched Jacobs take a mouthful of coffee and place the cup on his desk with a satisfied smile. This smile, he guessed, was one of relief that the necessary period of questions had been negotiated without anything of a personal nature having arisen. He watched him reach for a pile of documents in a wire tray.

'Now,' said Jacobs with sudden zeal, 'while I think of it, we need to make a number of decisions about the Anderson account and how to proceed on that development at Bentleigh.'

Martin listened to the answering machine's new message, from which his name had been banished, and readied himself to speak. He was thankful that he could simply say what needed to be said and hang up. Though part of him would have been happy to have a simple conversation with Sara, that now seemed impossible, and these wished-for trivialities somehow indecent.

What he had increasingly come to realise was that Sara had not only been his wife but his closest friend, that there was a whole range of issues and an accompanying vocabulary, sometimes intimate, other times quite child-like – all the vulnerabilities that only closeness lets be seen – which were now forever lost to him. He had also come to know that the moment they had fled his life was not, as might be expected, when the two men's mouths closed on each other that night in the Fasanenstrasse apartment, but some days before, when he had made a simple acquiescence, agreeing to stay on in Berlin the extra week. From that time onwards, he had lost the capacity to talk to her, and it was the absence of this speech he rued as much as anything.

'Hello, Sara, it's Andrew,' he began with his stilted tongue. 'I just wanted to let you know I'm back at Prahran. We should probably speak sometime about finances and that sort of thing, for you and Naomi.'

He had spoken it, his daughter's name, the first time in so many months – he who had embraced a life in which there was no reasonable space for her, he who had chosen this to be his punishment. Perhaps for a moment he had come to doubt the wisdom of such a judgment. Could it possibly be that he would never see her, never watch the changes moving through her? That someone else, through their love, their care and their attention, would become her father? But now that this decision had been made, how could it be undone? Now that this silence had descended between himself and Sara.

He snapped back from these thoughts, the telephone still in his hand. How long had he been standing there in silence like some nuisance caller? He went to give his ritual goodbye, but the words 'take care' were clearly out of place. There flashed through his mind a host of endings, most of which, grotesquely enough, were suited to a business letter. Without adding a word, he replaced the receiver on the handset.

He felt cheap. His behaviour appalled him. And the situation was, he knew, entirely of his own making. Then it came to him that Sara may well have been at home, standing above the machine, listening to him force out the message and then make a fool of himself with his silence, not wishing to speak to *him*.

Martin moved back to the foam-cushioned sofa and sat. Why, he asked himself – knowing full well the answer – was the cost of love this woman and this child? He stared at the room's single piece of art, a glass-framed Van Gogh – *Café de Nuit*. The title had been written below the reproduction. Above it, in even larger letters, was the artist's name. The stars were blotched, as if their executor would have greatly benefited from corrective spectacles.

23

If Alex Jacobs had, for whatever reason, chosen not to mention Von Ruhland or make any enquiry into Martin's personal life, virtually their entire conversation centring on matters of business, Belsey's invitation for dinner seemed specifically tailored for the gleaning of gossip.

'Welcome back, Andrew,' he said, beaming. 'Sorry about this disgusting weather — it's supposed to be summer. Still, you know Melbourne. Oh, before I forget, thanks for Marlene — she's been dutifully installed on the refrigerator door. Talking of which — refrigerators I mean, not Fräulein Dietrich — there's a bottle of the good widow Cliquot waiting to be liberated. It was a toss-up between that and a *Liebfraumilch*.'

'Stick with the older women every time,' said Martin.

Belsey headed for the kitchen annex, raising his voice as he went.

'Now, you must tell me everything about Berlin and how things are going with the mysterious Von Ruhland.'

Martin heard the popping of a cork and waited till his host reappeared with the bottle and two champagne flutes.

'Berlin's fine — actually Berlin was freezing when I left.'

'I've promised myself a trip as soon as the Sony City Filmhaus is ready — I can *wait* to visit the Dietrich collection. Here you are.' He handed Martin a glass of champagne. '*Prost!*'

'Yes, *Prost*,' Martin responded.

The two men took a seat at opposite ends of the leather couch.

'So how long are you back home for this time?' Belsey asked. 'I suppose there's not much keeping you here now.'

'Just a few friends —'

'All of whom no doubt pale into insignificance against the *Überarchitekt*. I'm still waiting to see a few candid shots. I keep imagining a cross between Rutger Hauer and Max von Sydow.'

He took a long drink of champagne and topped up both his and Martin's glass.

'I suppose with *your* reputation, you could more or less work from anywhere. Mind you, I was reading the other day that there aren't too many jobs for architects in Berlin any more. A few years ago they were in plague proportion. Now that the money's dried up, most of the projects are on hold. Of course, it's not only architects who are out of work. I believe they've got unemployment as bad as in the 1930s. All a bit ominous as far as I can see!'

'Where do you get all this information?'

'Off the toilet walls, my dear.'

Martin leant back on the couch and reached to his jacket pocket.

'Do you mind if I have a cigarette?' he asked.

'Cigarettes! Good Lord, hasn't the Hun led *you* astray.'

Martin brought out one of the packets he had purchased at Kyoto Station.

'What are they?' Belsey asked.

'Hope.'

'Do they work?'

'I hope so!'

Belsey stood up and walked to a cupboard where he ferreted amongst the bric-a-brac, emerging with a highly ornamental pedestal ashtray.

'This rather unfortunate object was a present from an admirer,' he explained, placing it to Martin's right. 'Talking of presents . . .' Belsey left his sentence unfinished and hurried over to a beechwood cabinet against the far wall. He retrieved a gift-wrapped package from the top and brought it over to Martin.

'Welcome home,' he beamed.

Martin edged the raffia ribbon from the package and unfolded the rice paper. Inside he found an old hardcover book bearing the title *Is Germany Incurable?*

'I think you'll find it indispensable.'

The young architect turned to the title page. The book was written by a Doctor Andrew M. Brickner and published in America in 1943.

'It's a psychoanalysis of the German people en masse,' Belsey explained. 'It shows how they manifest the classic characteristics of paranoia.'

Martin flipped through two short introductory notes, one, he noted, by Margaret Mead.

'"German Symptoms",' he read out loud from the contents page. '"Megalomania, The Need to Dominate, Persecution Complex, Projection and Retrospective Falsification . . ." Where on earth did you find this?' he asked.

'St Vincent de Paul.'

'"Nazis are Germans, The German War Cult." The headings are fantastic.'

'Now you can't say you haven't been warned,' said Belsey. 'If you ask me, Tacitus had it right – a united Germany could've defeated the Roman Empire. Look what they did to Varus.'

'Who's Varus?'

'Look him up in Tacitus.'

'Who's Tacitus?'

'A rather quiet Italian I took to bed a few times.'

'To be quite honest, *I* find the Germans a very hospitable people,' said Martin, taking a drink of champagne.

'What did Churchill say?' Belsey noted. 'The Germans are either at your knees or at your throat.' He paused a moment. 'Mind you, I wouldn't complain about being on *my* knees in front of a couple of Germans.'

Martin leaned forward and propped his cigarette in the pedestal ashtray. Belsey loomed in front of him with the champagne.

'Top you up?' he asked, pouring so that the mousse rushed to the brim of the glass, but no further.

'If I didn't know better, I'd say you were trying to get me drunk,' said Martin.

'You never know your luck in a big city.' Belsey returned to his seat. 'If we keep this up, you might just have to stay the night.'

'Belsey, enough!' said Martin, attempting to inject some lightness into his caution.

'But *dear*, now you're a fully paid up member of the

club, I was only trying to make you feel at home. Or did I hear it incorrectly when you said you'd had it off with the German?'

24

'I think he was half drunk by the time I arrived; there was an empty bottle beside the refrigerator. You know how he gets, he can't stop himself.'

Martin turned right on amber lights and headed north along Orrong Road beneath the overarching plane trees.

'I'm sure he would've been mortified the following morning,' Natalie consoled. 'He's probably terrified to call you.'

'If he remembers.'

'You two have known each other a long time, haven't you?'

'We met in high school.'

'That's a lot of history to give up for one indiscretion.'

'With Belsey, it's never *one* indiscretion! The problem is, ever since he heard about Johannes, it's like it's open season on me.'

Martin and Natalie were returning from an amateur production of *Oklahoma* in which Natalie's elder sister had a role playing Aunt Eller. The evening had come at Natalie's suggestion. Since his return, she had seen Martin as unhealthily preoccupied, disengaged from his immediate surroundings. He needed, in her words, to get out and about.

'Do you realise this was our first evening together?'

She had been tempted to use the term 'first date', feeling as she did that articulating a wish somehow brought it closer to reality. It was the power of prayer.

'I really enjoyed myself,' she said, 'even with that dreadful orchestra.'

'Yes,' he agreed. 'Even with the orchestra, especially the trumpeter.'

'I have to say I've wanted to do this for some time,' she admitted, knowing, with her street not far away, that these words would be the preface to an all too imminent farewell. 'Not that it would've been possible before – or appropriate of course.'

'No.'

Natalie reached down to gather her handbag and the light scarf she had folded on top of it.

'I know she didn't approve of me,' she said.

'She thought you were after me.'

'Well, I was, wasn't I – in a way.' She paused. 'It's just I'd never have done anything to destabilise your relationship.'

'I know that,' Martin replied. 'Though I'm not sure Sara would've agreed.'

'There *is* a certain irony in all this,' Natalie went on, staring ahead through the windscreen. 'Here you are going straight from one relationship to another and I don't even get a look in.' She gave a small laugh, trying to make light of it.

'I wish it were that simple.'

'You can't go left here any more,' Natalie suddenly

broke in. 'They've just changed the direction of the street. You'll need to go left at the lights and go round the block. Sorry,' she continued. 'You were saying?'

'I was going to say that if it *had* been like that, I mean going from one relationship to another, it would've been easier to deal with.' Martin pulled up at the red light and flicked on his indicator. 'When Johannes came into my life, it didn't in any way diminish how I felt for Sara.'

'But it damaged the practice of it, surely, which eventually comes down to the same thing.'

The lights changed and Martin turned into High Street, the wheels of his Peugeot straddling the tram tracks.

'Take the next on the left,' Natalie said.

There was a short silence broken only by her direction: 'And left again here.'

Martin pulled up outside Natalie's Edwardian, one-of-a-pair house.

'Coffee?' she asked.

He thought a moment.

'No, I think I'd better be heading home.'

They were presented with the task of finding some closure to the previous conversation – to have dropped it would have left the unpalatable taste of avoidance in their mouths. It was Natalie who salvaged the situation, finding a thread which could be positively pursued.

'What about Naomi? Are you seeing her?'

'Hardly at all now,' he said, and even that, he knew, a lie. 'Not for months, actually.'

'Even if things are bad with Sara, for whatever reason,

you still need to spend time with Naomi. She'll need reassurance that you still love her, and that *she* isn't the reason for the marriage breaking up.' There was a certain knowing sadness in her voice. 'You should ring Sara and make a time,' she said, 'or, if you can manage it, a couple of times. The longer you put it off, the harder it'll be. You don't want to lose your daughter as well.'

25

As a direct consequence of Natalie's advice, Andrew and Naomi spent their first day together in some five months. It was a period of time which had changed her significantly – not only was she taller and her hair now braided, but she was imbued with a new air of confidence. Many of Martin's opinions were contrasted with those of a Miss Cooper, and several girls with whose names he was unfamiliar – Gemma, Jerrah and Claire – featured prominently in her conversation.

'We don't sleep in the afternoons any more,' she informed him. 'And I've been sick. I had a very bad cough.'

They passed through the main gate of the Melbourne Zoo, beneath the sculpted families of kangaroos and polar bears standing high on their white columns, beneath the frieze's arklike procession of animals, beneath the word itself – the curved horizontal strokes of the Z, the interlocking ovals of the double O.

'Are there any animals you'd really like to see?' Martin asked as they waited in the queue for tickets.

Naomi considered his question for a responsible period of time.

'I'd like to see the goats and the donkeys,' she declared.

'I don't think they have goats and donkeys here, poppet.'

'Why not?'

'Because they're farm animals.'

Naomi thought about this a moment.

'Miss Cooper told us all about goats and donkeys.'

'That's great. So, what do you know about goats?'

'They have babies.'

'Is that all?'

Naomi nodded.

'And what about donkeys?'

'Donkeys live in the country.'

'Why's that?'

'Because the city is too noisy.'

'Look over there,' said Martin, crouching down beside his daughter and pointing to the top of a cage. 'That's a whistling kite. It's like a small eagle.'

'The eagle builds its nest in the air and when someone dies it comes down and eats them.'

'That's a vulture, poppet.'

'No, it's an eagle,' she insisted. 'And her babies eat people too!'

Now they moved slowly through the Great Flight Aviary, a cathedral of wire abandoned in a forest and now overrun by its dense vegetation. They passed along the raised wooden walkway in a hushed reverence until Naomi broke from Martin's side, running forward to retrieve a small off-white feather from the boards.

'This is for you, Daddy,' she said.

Martin thanked her and placed it for safe keeping in his top pocket. 'Do you want to have something to eat now?' he asked. 'Or do you want to see some more animals?'

'I want to see the hippo-pota-moose and the crocodile!'

They carried their lunch – hot dogs, chips and flavoured milks – out to the seating area in front of the kiosk.

'Why did you leave Mummy?' Naomi suddenly asked, taking Martin completely by surprise.

'It's a bit difficult to explain. It's an adult thing.'

'Don't you love her any more?'

'It's not that, poppet. I just can't *live* with Mummy any more.'

'Why can't you live with Mummy any more?'

Martin opened the car door for his daughter, taking the moment to look back at the slanted red bricks of the zoo wall, at the string of barbed wire curving its way above. His thoughts returned to Von Ruhland's description of the closing days of the war: of how the zoo, by then the centre of Berlin's best defended area, was badly hit, so that the following morning alligators and snakes could be found in the streets and monkeys of all descriptions in the trees. Martin thought once more of the emaciated elephant – Siam, the name came back to him –

wandering insanely around its compound, trumpeting without cease.

26

As Martin had predicted those weeks before in the living room of Von Ruhland's Berlin apartment, on a Monday early in April a registered letter arrived at his office from the Kyoto City Council. They were honoured to accept his design for the City of the Arts building in Kiyamachi-dori. Would he be able to attend a small ceremony with the mayor on the morning of Wednesday 14th of April, to be followed by lunch and a mid-afternoon press conference? Would he also be available for various meetings, inspections, and the like, which might occupy a number of days stretching over a two-week period from the date of the ceremony?

Martin slowly folded the letter. His first thought was to ring Von Ruhland – but not from the office. It was, he felt, of paramount importance that no-one should learn of the success of the design before his collaborator. Fortunately, Jacobs was away from the office that morning. Martin consulted his appointment book for the afternoon, and on his way out instructed the secretary to reschedule the solitary engagement for the following week.

It was only as the number 6 Glen Iris tram veered left, screeching from St Kilda Road into High Street, that it occurred to him how the time in Berlin would be around four a.m.

At six that evening he punched in Von Ruhland's number. He waited, imagining the single repeated tone echoing through the apartment, until it rang itself out.

It had been his habit over the preceding months to call the older architect at least once a week, but usually later at night before retiring to bed. Martin determined that he would wait until a more usual hour.

At ten o'clock he rang again, but with a similar result. It was clearly too late now to ring Natalie or Jacobs, even should he have wished to let them be the first to know the news. He would simply have to be patient.

However, when Martin arrived at work the following day, he was met instantly by Jacobs.

'Well, then?' he said, standing there loose-limbed and somewhat buffoonish. 'Good news?'

'About what?' said Martin.

'Come on,' Jacobs persisted. 'Jacqui told me there was a registered letter from Japan. That sounds like news to me.'

That evening, on every half-hour between six and ten o'clock, he tried Von Ruhland's number. Immediately after his last attempt he rang Natalie, telling her the news. Belsey, he thought, would find out soon enough, and besides, he found no pleasure in the thought of the man eagerly squandering the information for purposes of self-aggrandisement.

Shortly after ten-thirty, Martin found himself staring at the cream-coloured handset — he wanted, he admitted to himself, to ring his wife and his daughter; he wanted them to be proud of him. The young architect reached towards the telephone, touching its cold plastic, almost daring himself to make the call. But then, he reminded himself, his success amounted to no more than having carried through a piece of deceit; his role had been that of a mere accessory, some junior accomplice receiving praise under false pretences.

The absence of Von Ruhland from the apartment had disturbed the customary patterns. Something, he felt, had changed; something had happened of which he was unaware, and this change itself could be usual or quite extraordinary. When should he ring again? In this state of ignorance no interval was reasonable or inappropriate.

What followed was a time rife with speculation. In his mind he plotted out entire days for the older architect: at one moment he was at the counter of the nearby wine shop, Entrepôt du Vin, paying for a bottle of French champagne he had chosen in anticipation of their success; at another he stood showering in a Swiss hotel, having chosen to stay overnight after some ridiculously long meeting with his stockbroker the evening before.

Each failure to make contact caused Martin to revise the timeframe of his expectations, from at first a matter of hours, then inevitably mornings, afternoons and, all too quickly, whole days. By Thursday the young architect imagined Von Ruhland in some distant country, far from either Berlin or Kyoto, engaged in research – his enquiry into the various densities of shadow, for instance, came to mind, reassuring him. In the meantime he would content himself with the prospect of an unexpected call from Johannes, catching him the very moment when his vigilance had dropped.

But the end of that week saw him leave for Kyoto, some three days ahead of his appointment with the City Council.

Martin arrived at Osaka's Kansai airport shortly after eight o'clock on a Sunday evening. He had decided against making the train journey to Kyoto that same day, choosing instead to stay overnight at a nearby hotel.

So it was that a warm autumn Sunday morning in Melbourne became, with the intervention of some twenty-four displaced hours, a warm spring Monday afternoon in Kyoto. A fortuitous intersection of these seasons as though it were a single day, with its temperature and its slight breeze held that moment, uncertain as to which direction it might proceed. Or so it struck the young architect as he wheeled his suitcase across Hachijo-dori, towards the New Miyako Hotel.

Martin stood aside as the porter slotted a plastic card into the security lock beside the door; on the green flashing light, suitcase in hand, he backed his way into the ninth-floor room. Martin thanked him, wondering if, despite his travel book's opinion, he should offer a tip. But the young man was already making his way out the door, and besides, it came to him that apart from some insultingly low coins, the smallest denomination he had in his wallet was a 10 000-yen note.

He walked to the windows and looked out across the city – the buildings pale, subdued, their tonings from grey to sand with flashes of apricot and brown. What were they to his eyes, these irregular juttings, if not a bordered garden – a turbulence of stone, as yet unraked. For a moment he felt a familiarity with this place, a nostalgia, knowing the hand of it, with the lifeline and fateline of its two rivers drawn across its upturned palm.

Andrew Martin caught the central subway line to Shijo Station, emerging at Shijo-dori along which he walked into the heart of the central business district, his body exalting in the warmth of the mid-April day. He allowed himself to wander aimlessly through the large department stores – Diamaru, Hankyu and finally Takashimaya, in the basement of which he discovered a huge food market. He drifted amongst the floor of counters and stalls, open to any offered temptation – sampling the fermented cabbage or the sweet ginger, the radish slices, or sipping bitter green tea from a tiny paper cup.

He took a late lunch at the *okonomiyaki* stall, sitting at its narrow counter, watching the dish assembled on the hotplate – the pancake mixture and its ten other ingredients, from the shallots, the gourd and eggs to the ginger, beef and bonito flakes.

He emerged from these weatherless, even-lighted zones into the crowded pavements of late afternoon. A vast assembly jostled before him: shoppers encumbered by their clutch of cord-handled bags; sailor-suited schoolgirls; boys in their caps and stand-up-collar jackets, so many soldiers from another continent, another century; the bottle-blonded, bottle-tanned *kogal* girls dressed in tight jumpers and miniskirts, perched on the stilts of their shoes. A multitude set free in opposing directions by the birdcalls of the 'Walk' signs – the shrill chirrup or the cuckoo – east–west, north–south, weaving through the young men handing out slim packets of tissues which they fanned like card sharps: this elaborate theatre played out before the halted shining cars, before the waiting taxicabs with their white, lace-covered seats.

With every intention of returning to his hotel room, Martin continued his journey back along Shijo-dori, until a single-level shrine across the road provided passage for the lowering afternoon sun, its oranged light striking a minor intersection of the shadowed boulevard with rainbow promise. Surrendering to the sign, Martin turned down the narrow side street, permitting it to introduce him to a net of laneways and arcades, hectic with small shops.

Near the crossing of Teramachi-dori and Sanjo-dori – a main road in the days when the Emperor resided in Kyoto – he was halted by a *Jizo* shrine, its wall of stone figures draped with layers of red and white children's bibs.

As he stood there, spellbound by these unblemished cloths and the hundreds of enscribed wooden plaques attached to the opposite wall, a woman entered. Martin stepped aside but remained within the confines of the narrow space, watching her, determined that after she had gone he would himself follow whatever ritual he saw enacted there.

Some minutes later, once again alone in this place, he approached the offering box and let fall inside it all of his loose change. He grasped the thick rope made of its three intertwined cords – one of peacock green, another red, the third of white – and rang the bell, its dull note pulsing out into the arcade. What should he meditate upon at such a time, if not the vicissitudes of his recent life? He thought of his failed marriage, of his daughter, of Johannes, and he found himself praying for peace to rest upon them all and, were it possible, upon himself. It seemed to him then as if he had drifted into a sleep from which he now suddenly awoke. What was he to do, lest it all be undone? The woman had bowed and surely it was twice? And at some stage she had clapped her hands together loudly as if to wake the very gods. Would his hands be capable of waking them? What noise could stir them now, if the century's chorus of screams could not? And then, was it twice she had bowed again? He moved back through the shrine, keeping always one part of it within his sight, until the raucour of the narrow laneways snatched the moment from him.

Shortly after seven, with darkness now fully on the city, he ventured from the hotel in search of a meal. He waited for the pedestrian lights to change at Hachijo-dori, halted beside a lamppost thick with tattering sheets of coloured, tear-off cards on which appeared photographs of various semi-naked girls. He stared at the phone numbers – 641 6188, 525 5965 – at the small heart sign, at the English 'OK'.

Martin walked directly to the row of restaurants facing each other across the ground-floor arcade in the southwestern extension of the railway station. He gazed through the windows at the dark boxes and the plastic models of food they held – small roofless houses with many rooms, each containing one special object. Here the room for simmered acorn squash; here the room for night-dried sole; here the room for butterfish.

Sometimes, what seems to be misfortune can prove propitious in the longer term. So, Martin argued, Von Ruhland's continued absence from the apartment might well allow him to break the news from Kyoto and, better still, it came to him, after the ceremony itself. He would return from City Hall late afternoon or early evening. He would telephone the master architect, the very cheque in his hand.

'We won!' he would exclaim. 'It happened just as we always thought it would.' And he would fly out to Berlin on the first available flight. So beguiling did he find this narrative that when he rang Von Ruhland later that evening, he willed the phone to ring unanswered.

'Better Wednesday,' he told himself. 'Better Wednesday.'

27

'Mirai-o-sakidorishita sakuhin. A work of the future.'

There was generous applause from the select group assembled for the presentation ceremony at City Hall as Martin moved forward to accept a small plaque and an envelope containing the winner's cheque.

Late that Wednesday afternoon, the lunch and press conference over, he returned to the hotel. He went to the refrigerator and took from it one of the miniature bottles of spirits, a whisky. He poured half the contents into a glass, added some ice, and walked over to the window.

Martin stared out at the distant surrounding mountains, their mass browned by the overlay of evening air, by the fumes of the shining traffic, their edge reduced to a silhouette of torn, heavy paper. He let the netting fall from his hand.

Better Wednesday. The phrase came back to him. Except that now, having provided an appropriate rationale for this moment, he found himself fearful of its realisation. He looked at his watch – it would be nine-thirty in the morning in Berlin. He must, he knew, choose a time and not falter, berating himself over this pathetic display. He would ring now. If no-one answered he would wait patiently until the following evening; if Anke were to answer, he would ask her to pass on a message: Could Johannes ring Andrew in Kyoto. He reached for the book of matches beside the ashtray and noted the hotel's number on the reverse side.

Almost as soon as he hung up on the unanswered call, the telephone rang. On the other end was a man called Mike Hutchinson. He introduced himself as an Australian expatriate who had resided in Kyoto for the past fifteen years, making his living as a travel writer and by doing the occasional feature for the Melbourne *Age* and the *Sydney Morning Herald*. They spoke briefly – Hutchinson had unfortunately been unable to attend the press conference but was interested in writing a piece on the competition. If he was amenable, perhaps they could meet the following day in the foyer of Martin's hotel?

The young architect sat waiting near the reception desk, observing the various groups arrive and depart. In particular he loved the name-tagged Americans, with their bustle and their extraordinarily loud voices.

'Well, we're outa here,' a stocky woman wearing khaki shorts announced to the foyer, as if the foyer might be vitally concerned, and, with five other khaki-shorted women in tow, marched through the front door.

Martin watched as a man in his late thirties in the company of another man – tall, with somewhat unfashionably long hair and carrying what he took to be a camera box – moved aside to let the woman and her entourage pass by.

Martin stepped forward and made his enquiry.

'Mike Hutchinson?'

'Andrew Martin, how are you?'

The two men shook hands.

'And this is Chet,' Hutchinson announced, indicating

the tall man. 'I was hoping we could get a few photos today, perhaps at the construction site itself. If that's okay with you?'

The three men walked along Kiyamachi-dori, following the Takase and the rows of cherry trees and willows. The surface of the narrow river was smothered with blossom, a slowly moving pink mass.

'It was channelled into a canal early in the seventeenth century,' Hutchinson was explaining. 'You've probably seen the monument to Suminokura Ryoi at the front of the school – he's the man who did the work. This district used to be filled with shops supplying timber for pottery kilns and charcoal for cooking and heating.'

When they reached the empty school building, Hutchinson halted and turned his attention to the photographer.

'If you could get a few shots first up, Chet, then you'll be free for the rest of the day.'

Chet approached Martin and stood before him taking light readings. He moved back and examined his subject.

'Is there a problem?' Hutchinson called out.

'He doesn't look like an architect.'

'What do architects look like, for Godsake?'

Chet ignored the comment and continued staring at Martin. After a few moments he turned back to the journalist.

'Mike,' he called, 'could you go round to Maruzen and get me some large sheets of paper – anything'll do, so long as it rolls up easily. The bigger the better.' Chet turned his attention back to the young architect.

'Now,' he said, 'while we're waiting, I might get a couple of shots with you leaning over the bridge looking down the canal – like an idea's coming to you, you know. A bit serious.'

'I'll think *Death in Venice*.'

Following Chet's departure, Martin and Mike Hutchinson had taken lunch together at Pa Pa Milanos, an Italian restaurant just around the corner from the elementary school. Hutchinson had run through his questions – on Martin's rise to prominence, on his overseas engagements, and the philosophical underpinning of the Kyoto project, for which Martin had happily spelled out in more general terms his argument for the speaking-to-the-design session back in January.

Now the two men walked together towards the crowded corner of Kawaramachi-dori and Shijo-dori.

'Are you free tonight by any chance?' Hutchinson asked, checking his coat pocket for his notebook.

'What did you have in mind?'

'It might sound a bit odd coming straight after lunch, but how about dinner somewhere? Have you eaten at a *ryotei* – a traditional Japanese restaurant?'

'No,' said Martin, and hesitated a moment. 'There's someone I know in Berlin, a friend who spent some time in Kyoto. I remember him saying that you haven't truly experienced Japanese food, not only the cuisine but the tableware, until you've eaten it by candlelight. Do any restaurants here still use candles?'

'I doubt it very much,' Hutchinson replied. 'But I'll make some enquiries. Just don't get your hopes up, that's all.'

'I won't.'

'You've probably noticed, everyone here seems to eat early. I'll call at the hotel around seven. Yes?'

'Yes,' said Martin, sealing the pact.

'Now, unfortunately, I've got another appointment up north. You'll be right getting back?'

'Sure. I'll just walk down to Shijo Station and get the subway.'

'Okay then. I'll see you tonight at seven.'

'Looking forward to it,' Martin called to Hutchinson, who had already headed off into the crowds.

He waited with a pool of pedestrians at the lights, ready to head west along Shijo-dori. From his right, in the direction Hutchinson had taken, came an amplified voice, strident in its proclamations. Martin identified its source – a matte-black bus locked in the traffic some ten car lengths back along Kawaramachi-dori. The lights changed, but Martin stood his ground against the forward rush, holding his position until the first of the approaching crowd reached him. At this moment he turned to his right, cutting diagonally across their path, moving towards the ranting voice. He paused at the sidewalk's edge, some metres along the northbound street. From this vantage point he watched the funereal passage of the bus until it was beside him, its blackened windows hiding from view whoever it was who bellowed his words through the loudspeakers mounted on the roof – this black bus with its uniformed driver and its flank emblazoned with the image of the rising sun.

28

The waitress placed the next course before each of the two men and shuffled back on her knees towards the doorway. She bowed low to them and slid shut the panel of opaque paper.

Hutchinson had arrived at the hotel as promised and they had travelled by taxi to a *ryotei* off Imadegawa-dori. The young architect had found himself conducted down a low passageway to a room some three metres square, illuminated only by a large candle and the residual light coming from the Japanese garden onto which the space gave. He had no idea, nor would Hutchinson satisfy his curiosity, by what means and at what cost this particular arrangement had been procured.

'It took a bit of ringing around to find someone who'd cooperate,' the journalist had conceded. 'I think you'd need to go back to the thirties, maybe earlier, for something like this to happen as a matter of course.'

'Well, it's absolutely fantastic,' said Martin.

'Have you read Junichiro Tanizaki?'

Martin shook his head.

'You must read Tanizaki on shadows. Take the lacquerware for instance,' Hutchinson went on. 'Look at the gloss. How it broods. In normal light all of this would be lost. Here you can see how the red, the brown or the black are simply endless layers of darkness.'

Martin looked down at the shallow bowl in front of him, the way the tiny portions of fish seemed to have gathered the light towards them.

'And what about the rice,' Hutchinson asked, 'or the face of the woman who serves it?'

'This is sea bream and omelet shaped to form a single cherry blossom,' the journalist was explaining. 'It's the spring motif again.'

'And what's that next to it?' Martin asked, pointing to the other arrangement in the bowl.

'That's a Shinto wand used in purification rites. They've made it from ginger root, squid, and I think that's probably trout – it's a common spring menu fish.'

Hutchinson sought out a petal of bream with his chopsticks.

'So, what've been your impressions of Kyoto so far?'

'I was immediately struck by the flatness,' said Martin. 'You get the feeling that the city is actually restraining architecture.'

'Mind you, it's restraining less and less each year. It wasn't that long ago the council gave the okay to thirty- or forty-metre high buildings around the Shijo area. Then along comes Hiroshi Hara's new Kyoto Station, sixteen storeys high. Nearly everyone objected to that – even the Buddhists were worried it'd block their view of Toji

Temple and the landscape of the city – but up it goes. And then there's the Kyoto Hotel just near City Hall.'

'Yes, I've seen it.'

'And that's, what, fifteen storeys.'

'Even so, from an architectural point of view, Kyoto still strikes me as a very feminine city.' Martin paused. 'And what about you, after fifteen years of living here, what's your opinion?'

'To me, it's a city of immense melancholy,' Hutchinson replied. 'At Kyoto's heart there's an absence. It's the Imperial Palace waiting for the Emperor to return from Tokyo.'

After dinner, for which the journalist insisted on paying, Hutchinson suggested they go for drinks at The Metro, a nightclub inside the number 2 exit of Keihan Marutamachi Station. The two men found a seat at one of the round tables set against the side walls, diagonally facing a small stage in the back right-hand corner of the darkened room.

'So, the story goes, at lunchtime these girls would head to Kyoto Station, change from their school uniforms into something chic and erotic, and play the city. After an hour they'd get their uniforms from the lockers and head back to school. It got to the stage where there were advertisements for them on those packs of tissues they hand out in the city. You've seen them?'

'Yes,' said Martin, remembering that his own jacket pocket contained two of the very thing.

'They had a cellular phone number and some line like, Meet a Locker Girl, buy her fancy clothing, have sex.'

'It sounds quite remarkable in a city like Kyoto.'

Hutchinson took a long drink of his beer before offering, 'Perhaps it isn't true.'

'Where did you hear about it?' Martin asked.

'I read it in an architecture magazine.'

'Now you *are* lying!'

'Now I'm *not*,' Hutchinson protested. 'I'll send you a copy of the article.'

'I'll look forward to it. And if I'm free tomorrow lunchtime I'll have a wander around the locker rooms.'

They laughed. It was Hutchinson who broke the ensuing silence.

'Tonight's been the first genuine conversation I've had in a long while,' he said, adjusting his glass slightly on the table before him.

'I'm not sure what you mean by genuine,' Martin replied.

Hutchinson looked up somewhat wistfully.

'Chet's a nice guy, don't get me wrong, but he can't really talk. I mean he can talk about f.stops and megapixels, but he's no Derrida.'

'Rest assured, neither am I,' said Martin. 'When it boils down to it I just design buildings. *I* talk about CADs and horizontal planimetric space.'

'There's a difference – and you know it. And you don't "just design buildings". No ordinary person could've designed the City of the Arts building.'

Martin found himself silenced by the truth of Hutchinson's last remark. The journalist, however, read it as a type of pensiveness.

'A hundred yen for your thoughts,' he said.

'Very non-Derrida-like, I'm afraid. I was thinking I'd better be getting back to the hotel. I've got a day full of appointments tomorrow, starting at seven-thirty.'

'No worries,' said Hutchinson, downing the last of his beer. 'We can share a cab – the New Miyako's on the way to my place.'

The two men stood and pushed their chairs back under the table. They moved their way through the darkened room, back between the DJs' wire cages. At the door they were met by a number of teenagers dressed in the uniform of the band scheduled to play later that night. The teenagers stood aside to let them pass. Hutchinson paused just outside the poster-covered metal door and reached inside his jacket.

'Here's my card,' he said. 'I'd use the mobile number, it's safer.'

'Safer?'

'Chet never answers it.'

They took the taxi to the New Miyako. To the journalist's offer of ringing in a couple of days Martin had voiced no objection, feeling safe in the knowledge that he could avoid further contact by claiming an extremely busy schedule until a flight back to Australia would effectively cover his trail. He thanked Hutchinson for a good evening and told him how he looked forward to reading the article when it appeared.

Back in his room Martin walked immediately to the bathroom mirror and stared at his face, at his fine features – the long eyelashes, the high cheekbones. He would, he suddenly realised, be attractive to certain men. He wondered for how long this had been the case – the image he looked at in the mirror no longer seemed totally familiar. He stared at this face, at its soft beauty, and for the first time in his life he saw himself as others might, with desire.

Martin glanced down at his watch. Although he had made a promise to himself not to call again until the weekend, he moved back into the main room, sat down on the bed edge beside the telephone and entered the number of the Fasanenstrasse apartment. Only this time, for reasons that Martin himself could not explain, the oppressive silence behind the unanswered tone brought to his mind a fear he had kept long suppressed: that the architect was ill or had suffered some terrible accident and had been hospitalised. Or worse . . . And he knew the words but would not pronounce them, not even in his thoughts. He was, however, unable to keep from his mind an image of the apartment, dark and still, the furniture shrouded with large white sheets. He placed the phone back on the handset and reached for the cigarettes he had purchased the day before: Peace.

29

It was not until late in the following week that Martin had the opportunity of revisiting the building site. He had arranged to meet with a council officer, Yamakawa Ryo who would provide him with keys to the elementary school and grounds.

Martin had arrived earlier than expected. He stood once more before the building, his imagination enveloping the existing structure with the older architect's design. By their conspiracy, here would rise the first illicit monument to Johannes Von Ruhland, smuggled onto the Earth. Martin thought himself into the future when it would be revealed, perhaps even by himself as an old man, how he had secretly adorned the world with the creations of the master architect – buildings hand in hand with his own.

He walked to the empty playground and stared across the pale beaten earth – a barren, parchment-coloured expanse fenced from the street and walled beyond by the styleless backs of buildings.

Everywhere he could hear the calls of melancholy: the city crying for its absent heart; the site lamenting its own imminent passing, putting forth its vulnerable traces for sympathy – here the solitary climbing bars with their basketball hoops, here the worn approach to a side entrance. And what of his own melancholy at the silence of Von Ruhland, and the other silences of his previous life?

Ryo arrived in a taxi. He scurried across to Martin, apologising for his lateness.

'I was here early,' said Martin, seeking to put the young man at his ease. 'You were on time.'

Ryo bowed to the architect and thanked him.

'It is very beautiful here,' said Ryo, looking around. 'You have come at the right time for the cherry blossom.'

The two men walked side by side towards the main entrance to the building.

'I believe this street was once full of shops selling timber for the pottery kilns and coal for heating,' Martin said.

'Kiyamachi is "wood shop district". Yes, I imagine you are right. But I know nothing of the history of this place,' Ryo said. 'I am too young.'

They had begun to climb the five stone steps to the front door when Ryo's cellular phone clarioned out several bars of the *William Tell* overture.

Martin waited behind him on the steps, listening to a broken sequence of a single word – *hai, hai, hai*. At the end of the call, Ryo placed the keys to the building back in his pocket and turned to Martin.

'I have just received a call from Mr Nakanishi. Perhaps you will have met him?'

'Yes,' said Martin. 'After the presentation ceremony.'

'Yes. Mr Nakanishi wishes, if it is possible, that you come with me to City Hall as there is a matter he wishes to discuss with you. We can do this now?'

'Certainly,' Martin agreed.

'From here, we should perhaps walk to Kawaramachi-dori and find a taxi. This is quicker than taking a train and far more pleasant.'

Martin was met by two men: Mr Nakanishi and another whose name he could not catch.

'Mr Martin, please,' said Mr Nakanishi, indicating a chair. The two council officials took their seats opposite him. 'We are sorry for calling you from your work, but we felt it was necessary to talk with you as soon as possible.'

'That's fine,' said Martin.

Both men offered a small bow of the head.

'Only a few days ago,' said Mr Nakanishi, 'we had the pleasure of announcing you as winner of the competition for the Kyoto City of the Arts.'

'Thank you,' said Martin, by way of acknowledgment.

'More recently,' Mr Nakanishi continued, 'a letter was brought to our attention relating to this award.'

The man with the unknown name straightened the cover of a manila folder which lay in front of him on the desk, then turned his attention to Martin.

'The letter of which Mr Nakanishi has spoken,' he began, 'is from Herr Johannes Von Ruhland. It arrived yesterday morning, forwarded by our embassy in Berlin with a summary of its contents. We felt it appropriate to obtain a full and accurate translation.'

Martin leant forward at the sound of the architect's name, his pulse quickening. For him, Von Ruhland's previous silence now became intelligible. The older architect had come from years of self-imposed obscurity to add his voice – and what a delicious irony this would be – to the concert of praise for the competition-winning design.

'Herr Von Ruhland states that you were resident at his

apartment in Berlin from November of last year until January of this year.'

He raised his eyes to Martin, seeking a response. Martin nodded, then felt under an obligation to actually voice the word: 'Yes.'

'He goes on to state that the plans for the City of the Arts submitted under your name were based on his original design and presumably copied by yourself in an attempt to disguise their origin.'

Martin found it impossible to make a direct response. They had been discovered – their plot was suddenly and unexpectedly revealed – but only through this inconceivable self-betrayal. These were his first thoughts, swiftly followed by how this might be misconstrued as a criminal act perpetrated by himself alone.

'I'm sorry, there must be some mistake,' he said, his heart racing. It struck him that if this should be the case, his only defence would be to break the very confidence he had sworn to uphold. Martin watched the man whose name he did not know turn the cover of the manila folder and remove a sheet of paper.

'You say there is a mistake, Mr Martin. We would be most happy to find this is so. But first, perhaps you would be so kind as to examine this letter.'

He leant forward and handed the sheet to Martin.

The first thing the architect recognised was the paper, its weight, then the embossed address in Fasanenstrasse. His eyes half blindedly scanned the page, taking in the familiar gothic script. He forced himself to concentrate.

It was then he saw what he had already been told, that the letter had been written in German. He stared at the incomprehensible words, suddenly feeling his vulnerability, realising how alone he was in this place with these other cultures gathering, it seemed, against him, with their languages he could not speak, graphic traces he could not read.

Mr Nakanishi pointed to the bottom of the page.

'That is the signature of Johannes Von Ruhland?' he asked.

'Yes.'

'You know it well?'

'Yes.'

'Perhaps then you might comment on the assertion made by Herr Von Ruhland that the plans as submitted were of his invention?'

'That is true,' Martin answered. 'The plans are those of Johannes Von Ruhland.'

Mr Nakanishi's head rose as though sprung back. The two men sat in silence for perhaps thirty seconds. Then they consulted, *sotto voce*, in Japanese.

'Let us be clear,' Mr Nakanishi continued. 'You are saying that you copied these plans and submitted them under your own name?'

'Yes,' he replied. 'I copied them and then I submitted them under my name.'

There was another long pause.

'Mr Martin,' the other man said. 'You spoke a moment ago of there being some mistake. Would you be so kind as to explain to us the nature of this mistake, especially in the light of your most recent comments?'

30

Martin chose to return directly to Australia. There was, as Mr Nakanishi had said shortly before the conclusion of the meeting, nothing compelling him to stay in Kyoto. No-one from the council, he was at pains to point out, was intending to lay charges against him. They were of the unanimous opinion that the best design had been chosen and would liaise directly with Von Ruhland about its realisation. The issue of plagiarism, Mr Nakanishi suggested, was something to be resolved between the two architects. Apart from that, there was only the matter of returning the preparation fee and winner's cheque.

Martin left his suitcase just inside the front door of his flat, dumped the weekend papers on the sofa and walked reluctantly to the flashing answering machine. As he'd feared, the news of his success in Kyoto had travelled quickly outwards from Natalie and Jacobs, eventually blurring into the field of vague acquaintances and forgotten business contacts. Martin forwarded through the words of congratulation which now served no purpose other than to heap irony upon irony.

He skipped through the last messages, then went straight to the bedroom. Undressing clumsily, he piled his clothes on top of each other across the arm of a chair, and climbed into bed.

That evening, with an increasing sense of desperation, Martin tried Von Ruhland's number yet again. He hung up, then dialled for some home-delivered food. He had no particular appetite and knew his order to be a distraction from the unpleasant reality in which he found himself. He pulled a bottle of red wine from its storage place at the bottom of the bedroom's built-in wardrobe and poured himself a glass. He spent some time unpacking, then sat at the coffee table with the first of the weekend papers: a front page which spoke of continued massacres in Timor, and a NATO rejection of a Milosevic peace plan.

Twenty minutes later he was staring at his own image on page three of the *Saturday Extra*. He saw himself striking an affected pose before the elementary school, a roll of white art paper in his hand. He began to read the article itself.

> Andrew Martin sat at a table in one of Kyoto's trendiest night spots – host to the notorious *sutoreito janai yoru* or 'not straight night' – The Metro. Martin had cause to celebrate. Just recently the bright young man of Oz architecture was chosen from amongst the world's best in a competition to design a City of the Arts right in the centre of the geisha district.

He read on, watching as Hutchinson's article meticulously painted its picture of a gay high flyer, smartarsed and opinionated.

The doorbell rang. It was a dusky-faced young man with a home-delivery 'for Martin'.

Two days later the newspapers carried the story he had brought home with him from Kyoto – another tall poppy could be cut down to size. His name, he knew, would once again be on everyone's lips. 'The Martin position' was now ripe for jokes.

The young architect looked down at the photograph of his face. It appeared to be a blown up detail from the portrait in the Saturday feature. He brought the image close – his features were reduced to a series of dots like some frightful outbreak of acne.

Jacobs was at the front door, both furious and distraught.

'Have you gone completely mad?' he said, without so much as a greeting. 'Do you realise what's going to happen to the practice when people realise *you're* the Martin in Jacobs, Martin & Co.?'

'I've a pretty good idea,' he replied flatly.

'So have I!' Jacobs stormed his way inside. 'If I were a sporting man, I'd land one right on your nose for this.'

'Well, at least I'm safe there, aren't I.'

'It's hardly a laughing matter, Andrew – it could be the end of the company.'

'Can I suggest you buy me out,' Martin said, closing the front door. 'Disown me and get in another partner. That's the best thing you can do – denounce me in public.'

'I'll need to stand in the queue.'

'Then do it. Wait your turn and put the boot in.'

'For Godsake, Andrew, will you stop being so bloody cooperative. I came here to abuse the hell out of you. Don't take that away from me too!'

Jacobs sat down on the sofa. The aging foam compressed beneath him.

'What's the problem with the sofa?' he asked.

'It's old and cheap. It came with the flat.'

Jacobs looked around the room, his eyebrows raising involuntarily.

'Andrew, what's happened to you? Ever since the Berlin conference, you've seemed to be hell-bent on self-destruction. There was all that unfortunate personal stuff, and the running backwards and forwards around the globe – not that it's any of my concern – but really, to pinch Von Ruhland's ideas and hope to get away with it is a bit much.'

'I didn't "pinch" his ideas, Alex.'

'Well, what do you call it – a loan? A heavy influence?'

Jacobs went to lean forward on the sofa, but found it impossible.

'Why on earth did you do it? That's what I can't understand.'

'If I told you,' said Martin, 'you wouldn't believe me.'

'Try me.'

'I can't tell you, Alex. It would be breaking a confidence.'

'We're facing bankruptcy and you're talking moral philosophy? Come on, Andrew, you owe me more than that.'

Martin stood there a moment, considering.

'You swear to me, not a word of this to anyone? Not your wife. No-one.'

'Yes, of course.'

'I want you to swear it, Alex. I know it might sound preposterous to you, but I'd like you to actually say the words: "I swear I won't tell anyone."'

'And do you want me to cross my heart and hope to die as well?'

'Alex, please.'

'I swear I won't tell anyone,' Jacobs enunciated with as much dignity as he could muster.

Martin sat down on the sofa at the opposite end to Jacobs. The opportunity to say these things out loud, for them to be heard, was in itself an immense relief.

'It's true that Von Ruhland did the designs,' he began, 'but he asked me to redraft them electronically, do some computer modelling, and submit them under my name.'

Jacobs sat there dumbfounded for some seconds.

'That's it?' he eventually said. 'That's your story?'

'In essence, yes.'

Jacobs shook his head, almost in despair.

'Jesus, Andrew. Do you expect me to swallow this? If he's set you up, why haven't you said anything? Denounce him! Why don't you simply denounce the man?'

'Because I gave my word. Because I love him.'

A look of mild disgust spread across Jacobs' face.

'The fellow wrecks your career – not to mention the

other business, your marriage, I mean – and you tell me you love him!'

'There's been some mistake, that's all. I just need to speak with him about it and it'll all be cleared up.'

Jacobs stared at him, momentarily stunned into speechlessness.

'You don't believe me, do you?' Martin said.

'Andrew, I'm simply looking at the facts.'

After Jacobs left, the young architect moved to the telephone. He stood there, the long note of the German ringing tone keening in his ear.

31

He had been waiting for the visit from Belsey. Their relationship had been considerably strained after the last meeting, and Belsey's apologetic phone call had failed to emerge. Martin was correct when he guessed that Belsey would wait until he had some official business to conduct before making contact again.

Unlike Jacobs, Belsey did not bother to sit down; he obviously was neither hoping for nor expecting a long visit.

'The institute's striking you from the membership,' he said with the tone of a headmaster. 'I expect you've seen this coming. There's a letter in the mail from the committee. I thought I'd at least let you know in person.'

'I appreciate that, Belsey,' Martin said, the reasonableness in his own tone nearly choking him.

'This is deeply embarrassing to me, Andrew. You gave

me absolutely no room to speak in your defence, which I think the committee expected, given our closeness.' He paused. 'Have you heard anything from the Registration Board?'

'Not yet,' Martin offered matter-of-factly.

Belsey nodded. He started to move for the door.

'I can't imagine what possessed you to do such a thing! I mean, did you seriously think you'd get away with it? You of all people would know an architect's signature's in every line, computer-assisted or not. Unless you thought with Von Ruhland being so far away and so obscure —'

'In my eyes, I've done nothing wrong,' Martin interrupted.

'I'd get my eyes tested, old son!' said Belsey. 'The evidence is there for everyone to see. If you were innocent, this would never have happened. You've been caught red-handed and, frankly, if you get away without some legal proceedings, you'll be damn lucky. I tell you, at this time I wouldn't be in your shoes for the world.'

'Is that it?' Martin said. 'I've been through this already with Jacobs — I don't want to go through it again.'

'Yes, I suppose it is,' said Belsey. 'Well, I'll be going then.'

He opened the door himself and stepped out onto the landing. Before leaving he offered some final advice.

'I think the best thing you could do is to write to Von Ruhland and apologise. At least that. I think it might make you feel better.'

32

'It's like he's hiding from me,' Martin lamented. 'And all I've done is what he asked me to do.'

He stood, hands clenched in frustration, opposite Natalie Vlies in his Prahran flat.

She quietened him, told him to sit down whilst she made some coffee. Only then did she reopen the issue.

'I've heard all these rumours and half-truths,' she said, 'most of which don't make much sense given the Andrew Martin I know. I'd just like to hear your side of the story.'

'Johannes asked me to submit his plans under my name,' he gabbled out, like a prisoner breaking down under interrogation. 'That's all I did.'

'No,' she jumped in, halting him. 'I want the whole story, not just the end.'

And so Martin began systematically reconstructing the chain of events, a steady chronological unfolding, with no reordering for whatever effect. When he had finished, or rather when he stopped, for he had not told everything, Natalie had her first question ready.

'Why did you keep this a secret – from *us* I mean, from the people you trust, especially before the result was announced?'

'You know how news travels in this business; I didn't want to compromise the chances of Johannes' design coming to fruition. There's no building of his on Earth, did you know that? If only you'd seen what I saw in Berlin, the designs . . .'

'But surely if Johannes Von Ruhland truly wanted his

works realised, he'd have no trouble – especially if they're as astounding as you say?'

Again, the logic that seemed to pertain in Berlin had no value here. His silence was cut through by Natalie's elaboration.

'You can't seriously believe that in this day and age his work would be shunned because once he was a member of the National Socialists? I mean, at that time, practically everyone in Germany was.'

'That was what he told me – I didn't question it.' Martin paused, then made a small qualification. 'No, that was how he said it was immediately after the war. I didn't question how things might be different now. There seemed to be no need.'

Natalie shook her head. She shifted the line of her questioning, each new tack addressing an issue he had failed to consider, raising doubts he dared not speak.

'What about you?' Natalie was continuing. 'Why did *you* do it?'

'Sorry?'

'Why did you go through with the deceit – submitting the plans in your name?'

'Because he asked me.'

'And it never struck you as strange?'

'Not then. Not there.'

'And not here either?' Natalie allowed herself the moment of breath for emphasis. 'Unless you didn't *want* to see how odd it was,' she said. 'Unless you were doing something like punishing yourself.'

'For what?'

'You tell me. For destroying your marriage? For having sex with a man?'

'Andrew,' she'd said. 'You don't have a choice any more.'

It was after midnight. Natalie had long since gone but Martin remained in the lounge room, turning over in his mind her words from that evening.

Exposing Von Ruhland was simply out of the question. There had been a pact between them. He had given the older architect his word.

'And he didn't give his?' Natalie had asked. He had wished to let it pass, that difficult question.

'No,' he'd said at last.

'Andrew, you're being totally destroyed by this business.' And she had stood, by way of underlining it: 'You don't have a choice any more. You have to make some sort of public statement.'

Outside, the rain which had started only minutes after Natalie had left continued to teem, lashing hard against the lounge-room windows. He heard Natalie's plea again — he must denounce Von Ruhland.

But Martin knew that to give the necessary weight to this denunciation he would need to thoroughly discredit him. He must paint the older architect as a Nazi directly involved in the processes of genocide; he would need to tell of the Cleansing Centre. And to reveal that would be the ultimate breach of trust. In all he had said in his time with Natalie, it was the one thing of which he had not spoken, for this deepest secret, and the moment of its telling, he knew, was Von Ruhland's declaration of love.

Now, alone again in this single-bedroom flat, with several whiskies having taken their toll, the question arose in his head: why would Von Ruhland have chosen to destroy the one he loved? Did he believe the younger architect had denied him, or deserted him in some way? But what had he done? Natalie's conjecture about another question – why Von Ruhland had stubbornly maintained his silence – returned to him.

'Is it possible he was angry at you for having come back here?' she'd asked. 'Is he jealous? Does he have doubts, like we do?' And then her more brutal enquiry: 'Do you actually *know* this man you say you love?'

What Martin did know was how he had resisted all temptations to expose Von Ruhland's complicity. He had been faithful. He had done nothing to put that love in jeopardy. In these matters he knew he could hold firmly to his innocence.

So it was that Martin found himself trapped in a state of suffering, the alleviation of which could be attained only by compromising his own sense of integrity and by breaking the most intimate bond between himself and the architect. The person he loved had caused this suffering and the only escape was to destroy him. Martin's own moral position could only now be maintained at the cost of this pain. Each day he floundered in these irresolvable situations, unable to act, without defence, and open to ridicule.

At one stage he came close to prayer, calling on the God of Victims, whom Johannes himself had aptly proven could not come to his aid. Not now. Only after his death. After all of their deaths.

Von Ruhland alone, he knew, could extricate him from this misery. And the architect remained silent.

As the weeks passed, Martin became increasingly reclusive. He no longer saw his child, feeling his presence to be a form of contamination. He no longer worked, bar the occasional small project Jacobs, as much out of convenience as guilt, let fall his way. He began in earnest the inevitable erosion of his savings and investments.

He now largely ignored the calls from Natalie, merely monitoring them through his answering machine. When her tone became concerned he picked up the phone as a means of ensuring she would not visit. He was fine, he'd say. No, nothing was wrong with him, and yes, he was eating well. All he needed was time and a temporary solitude.

Such meagre and obsessively repeated activities accounted for the winter and beyond. They passed, these months, and with them any hope of Von Ruhland coming to his aid. For his part, Martin no longer even bothered to ring.

33 One afternoon in early spring the young architect opened the door to reveal Sara. He showed her in, noting how her gaze quickly took in the room, assessing the circumstances of his life apart from her.

His own eyes followed that same path and he saw the furniture once again as others would see it – cheap and totally lacking in taste.

'I've come about the maintenance payments, given the . . .' and she paused over the word, '*uncertainty* of your future. I don't want this to take forever.'

She handed him an envelope. 'I've had a proposal drawn up by my solicitor. You could have a look at it over the next couple of days and get back to me.'

'Yes,' he managed.

'I also think it's time we did something officially about a divorce.' She was silent a moment before continuing. 'It's not fair on Naomi to be without a full-time father.'

'And what has that got to do with divorce?'

Again she paused.

'I've met someone – Alan. I'm seeing him, as they say.'

'I see.'

'Actually, he's waiting for me in the car downstairs.' And she added, 'I don't think *he's* queer.'

Then nothing. They stood there staring at each other, broken.

'Do you love him?' Martin asked.

'Who?' And it came to her the person he meant and what he meant by asking it. 'Alan?' she enquired, knowing it unnecessary.

Martin repeated the name, confirming it.

She waited a moment – barely that, a second – before she replied.

'I *loved* you.'

She turned, holding back the quickly rising tears, and started to the door. Then, her hand already gripping the doorknob, she turned a final time.

'I said I loved you. But that person who came back from Berlin wasn't you. Any more than this . . . *plagiarist* is you. Someone I used to love has disappeared and all that's left is a stranger with his appearance.'

She opened the doorway, walked out to the landing and closed the door on him.

By October Martin had made a choice. He telephoned Natalie, not for her opinion or advice, but simply to hear his own decision spoken aloud. And who else, in any case, could he ring, abandoned as he felt he was by all others?

'I'm going back to Berlin,' he said. 'I'm going to find him, wherever he might be. If I turn up on his doorstep he'll have to see me. He'll have to tell me why he's done this thing.'

Natalie's response was brief.

'If you ask me,' she said, 'the way he's abandoned you shows he's completely indifferent to what might be happening in your life.'

But where else could he turn other than to Von Ruhland? The Berlin apartment was the only place on Earth where his innocence and his faithfulness could be unequivocally known. Martin knew that the older architect alone could restore order to this world.

34

Martin had booked a room at Am Zoo – a mid-range hotel within easy walking distance of Von Ruhland's apartment.

He slept off some of his post-flight lethargy, waking around three in the afternoon. Then he showered, dressed, and set out down Ku'damm. He walked along the tree-lined boulevard, past the glass-sided display cabinets set in the centre of the broad sidewalks: here a poster for the film *Jakob der Lügner*, here a display of lingerie from Anna Dessous. He continued past the Gasthaus Aschinger with its colour reproductions of *6 Rostbratwürste, Fleischrippchen* and *Schnitzel 'Wiener Art'*, past the street stall selling Russian dolls and Russian hats, past the stall with cheap jewellery directly opposite Bucherer's jewellery store.

As he waited for the lights to change at Fasanenstrasse he was approached by a man in his fifties dressed in a camel-hair coat.

'*Entschuldigen Sie bitte!*' the man said. '*Ist hier eine Telefonzelle in der Nähe?*'

Martin stammered back a reply, half-English, half-German.

'Sorry,' he offered, '*Ich spreche kaum Deutsch.*'

The two laughed a moment together, then the man in the camel-hair coat offered his apologies, adding a parting remark in German, and moved off with a wave of his hand.

The young architect crossed Ku'damm, his face bathed in the burnt-apricot hue of the autumn afternoon sun – the bushfire light of Australia – and headed down Fasanenstrasse.

It was only as he stood there, before the building which contained Von Ruhland's apartment, that the long-suppressed thought surfaced that the architect might indeed be dead. He was in fear, as he had been the first time he visited, that the door might open to a stranger's face, and this only chance of restoring his life would be gone.

He rapped on the door and waited. When it opened shortly afterwards to reveal Anke, Martin – the weight of these months finally taking their toll – burst into tears.

Almost an hour passed, in which Martin slowly shook the burden of his unknowing from his body, wave after wave shuddering through him, exhausting him to stillness. For her part, Anke knelt beside him, showing no astonishment at such outpourings, as if they might be quite usual given what she knew of life. When he could stand, when he could properly walk, she led him to the bathroom and bathed his face in cool, scented water. She listened to his breathing as it slowed and knew that speech would soon be possible.

The questions came not long after, when he was seated in the kitchen watching Anke busy herself with making coffee as she had first done for him almost a year before.

'Does he know I've been trying to contact him?' he asked.

'I have no idea. All I know is he's been very preoccupied with other things.'

'I've been trying to contact him for months!'

'You have been ringing here?'

Martin nodded.

'Then I'm not surprised. I've only been here myself for the last couple of weeks. Johannes has been at Potsdam, at the summer house, since early April, perhaps longer. He's been conducting all of his business from there.'

'You've spoken to him?'

'Of course. I rang as soon as I got back from München.'

'And he's all right?'

'Yes. As I said, he's engaged in some new project.'

'Do you know what's happening with the City of the Arts building?'

'Nothing, as far as I know.'

'What do you mean, nothing?'

'He's not going ahead with it. He's told them he doesn't want it built. He says he has other, more important work that totally subsumes the project in Kyoto.'

What energy Martin had mustered for this visit seemed to drain away – all of this chaos, this disruption, this ruination of his life had been for nothing. The terrible doubt came to him: had Von Ruhland *ever* wanted this building realised?

'I must see him,' he said. 'Have you his phone number?'

'I've sworn not to give it to anyone.'

'Whereabouts is the summer house? I'll go there.'

'He said he didn't want to be disturbed for any reason.'

'Not me?'

'He told me, no-one.'

'But *you*, you could ring him. You could pass on a message, persuade him.'

Martin could hear the desperation in his own voice; he sounded like some imploring beggar.

'Can you talk to him for me? Ask him? One meeting, that's all I ask. Can you do that?'

The telephone rang.

Since his visit to the Fasanenstrasse apartment three days before, Martin had chosen to remain in his hotel room. Feigning an illness, he had arranged to have food brought to him in the evenings.

These days were measured out by sounds. The distant rumble of trains moving to and from Zoo Station; incomprehensible fragments of conversations snatched from passers-by beyond his door; and, beneath everything, the constant cascade of the fountains in the hotel's central courtyard.

It was Anke.

'He will see you,' she said.

'Thank God,' Martin uttered. 'What time? Where do I go?'

'Tomorrow afternoon,' she said. 'Now, do you know Potsdam at all?'

35

The two seats opposite and the four seats across the aisle were filled with tourists going to Potsdam to see the palace, Sanssouci – a cluster of Americans reading aloud their travel guides to each other.

'"Sanssouci was designed for Frederick the Great by his friend Georg Wenzeslaus von Knobelsdorff." Hey, that was a mouthful.'

'Good Georg Wen-zes-laus looked out, sear-ching for Sans-sou-ci . . .'

'He makes a song and dance about everything, I tell you.'

'I'm working on a rhyme here, Frank – Lucy, juicy –'

'Floosie!'

'That's not a true rhyme, Pat.'

Martin turned his face to the window and watched the autumn forest streak by – poplars and birches, a wash of bright yellow and burnt orange interspersed with flashes of reddish brown. Now a trunk brightly greened with moss. Here a stand overrun with mistletoe. The stations Nikolassee and Wannsee.

'"It was to be a palace . . ." Are you all listening? This is for your edification. "It was to be a palace *without cares* –"'

'That's *sans souci* in French, in case you didn't know.'

'Can someone put a bag on Jerry's head!'

'". . . a retreat where the King could escape the problems of the world".'

'If I remember it well, Voltaire visited the palace.'

'I'm coming to that, Jerry.'

Martin glanced back inside the carriage, focusing his eyes on the grey floor with its speckled pattern; it looked as though a wedding had been held here and the whole area strewn with confetti. He heard the potted histories continue, anecdote heaping upon anecdote.

'"Frederick the Great had the town houses of Potsdam embellished with grand façades, often using his own designs, behind which lived humble citizens . . ."'

Martin swung his view back through the window. He felt he was being drawn into the past. A past where many others before him had become trapped. The station Babelsberg. The old houses and shops densely scripted with graffiti, like so many calls for help.

The platform was suffused with the odour of hot bread and cheese from the *Ditsch* stall. Martin passed it by, moving through the construction work for the new Potsdam Station – to his left a passageway, its shops hidden behind thick plastic sheeting; here a section sealed off with red and white tape as if it were the site of a recent crime. He made his way through the large revolving doors at the main entrance into a wide open light; the taxi rank was almost directly in front of him.

Martin showed the hastily written address to the driver. Anke had given him general directions to the villa and a specific number in Am Neuen Garten. The cab made a wide U-turn and, following the tram tracks, headed right, over the river and through the town centre, continuing north along Friedrich-Ebert-Strasse. Shortly after, it veered into Am Neuen Garten, its tyres slapping on the old cobblestone surface.

Surely it will not be this, he thought. He stared ahead through the windscreen at a derelict, double-storey stuccoed villa. A building to all intents uninhabitable and uninhabited.

Martin watched the taxi drive off back down the street. He had been unable to explain how he wished it to simply wait for a few minutes whilst he explored this unlikely destination. Instead, the driver had insisted on the fare, pointing to the meter as though Martin were arguing about the amount.

As soon as he entered the grounds his view of the flanking villas was snatched from him by dense foliage. Before him, a circular driveway had sunk beneath layers of leaves. Surely, he thought, Anke must have given him the wrong street, or the wrong number. It was only because the recent year had shaken his belief in what might or might not be possible that he was persuaded to at least walk round the property in its entirety.

He made his way down the right-hand side of the villa, picking a path carefully through spongy ground riddled with mole-holes. He paused; just ahead the lower part of the wall had been brutally demolished by an explosion close to where, given the presence of some stone steps, he assumed a side entrance had once been. Martin mounted the first few of the steps and peered into the villa's interior. The room ahead was empty, a barren space giving a glimpse of a broad staircase beyond. The floor was littered with rubble; wires hung down from the roof. A grey-red dust from the pulverised bricks and plaster moved through the room as if recently disturbed.

Martin continued down the side of the villa, approaching a low doorway beside which there was a single word of Russian painted on the stucco in a childlike hand, and below it the abbreviation 'KB 1–6'. He looked down at the ground, ready to make his way onwards. Around the step of the door there were mushrooms growing, slender-stemmed with flat, coinlike crowns.

As he neared the back of the property the earth became firmer beneath his feet. He could see a broad swathe of land, largely overtaken by a weedish grass, beyond which the view was lost in thick stands of trees – poplars, birches, elms. Only as Martin turned at the far back corner of the villa did he see Von Ruhland, standing alone and perfectly still, enraptured, it appeared, by some vision.

'Johannes,' he called.

Von Ruhland cocked his head as though listening to a distant sound.

'Johannes,' Martin called again.

Von Ruhland turned slowly towards him.

'Yes?' he said.

It was as if the older architect were in the presence of a complete stranger. He gazed inquisitively at the person before him, then turned away, back towards the trees.

'Why?' Martin said to his averted face. 'Why did you do it?'

It seemed rather that the wind answered his question –

at first a distant flurry amongst the poplars, and then, amidst that quivering, a sudden gust bending the tree tops, discovering patches of fallen leaves and hurrying them through the grass.

'I did what you asked me to do,' he continued. 'That was all. Why did you ruin me?'

A sudden stillness overtook the garden. Von Ruhland began a second turn towards the young architect, so slow that Martin found himself afraid lest the face be distorted enough to stop his heart.

But what was revealed, this time, drew its limits at indignant fury.

36

'Who are *you*, defiling my activities with your questions and your ill-informed opinions?' He looked Martin up and down.

'Can you draw the line that I draw, with nothing but a knowledge of the myriad points of this world to join them with perfect straightness?' Von Ruhland stepped closer, the leaves scattering before him. 'Let your computers dare this with their piddling calculations worthy of a sweet-shop attendant licking his pencil lead!'

He was now only inches from Martin's face. The young architect could feel the fine spittle settling against his cheek.

'Can you draw the arc where every part of the curve is a curve, which if magnified a thousand times over would give you that same curve to magnify? Can you sleep and find that the hand alone has finished this line or this arc?

'You come here from God-knows-where to question *me*. What gives you the right to do that? Was it *your* imagination that conceived the wire palace of Salzburg or the angelic cages at Madras? Was it *you* who dreamt the Stockholm auditorium, its water panels reassembling the horizon to reset the sun each evening on five occasions?'

As the litany of descriptions began to grow, so did the force of the wind, a gathering turbulence slowly encompassing the whole garden, the leaves blotting out the air.

'What of the cathedral at Lourdes with its thousand steps, each stone eroded to the appropriate magnitude of sin? Each stone with its steepening concavity, upwards and upwards towards the final steps – lath, tissue, cellophane, gnat-wing, gossamer – all the degrees of thinness until the final step, which appears only as though it were a shadow on the one previous.

'And what of the motion buildings – the drifting hotel off Lecce? The ferris apartments in Wien? Are you familiar with their engineering? Or the combination of materials to withstand such pressures? And what of the cyberchambers? I could go on, yet a month would not see me finished, nor a year.'

Another barrage of wind buffeted Martin's clothes, clamouring at his half-turned body – shank, buttock and shoulder – forming this posture of contrition despite the warring emotions inside his heart.

'What was that? I didn't quite catch your answer,' Von

Ruhland bellowed out derisively. He stepped back and the very air fled from him, air of such velocity that Martin was forced to avert his face in order to breathe. The younger architect had now turned towards the back wall of the villa, its stucco surface riddled with bullet holes, the lower windows glassless, the bottom sills tufted with weed. He pulled his coat collar high, covering his face from the grit-filled air.

And now the older architect was hard against him once again.

'You come here with your maudlin tone, with your pathetic belief in your own righteousness! Do you believe your opinions make any difference to the scheme of things? You, with your sentimental dream of a world in which each receives according to his merit! Stand up like a man, and let me question *you*!

'Do you have any idea what you are interrupting with your pathetic notions of fair play? Do you imagine this is a public school, with you in a chalk-marked field bleating at the injustice of a referee's decision? What is the matter? Has my accuser swallowed his tongue?'

Martin looked up at the older architect.

'I've said too much already,' he gasped, raising his face from his coat. 'There's no point in me saying it again. I'll add nothing.'

'That is right. It is not for you to talk, it is for you to *listen*!'

The air began to column, routing through the leaf-thick earth. Von Ruhland bent his head back, swinging his view across the open sky. His face whitened, then purpled.

'It comes to me that I have talked only of buildings. But what of the city? What of the boulevards and squares? And then the gate and all that waits outside, the spreading suburbs where the crowds stroll ceaselessly? And beyond the suburbs – what of the patternless forests and the rivers flowing their own courses? The hinterlands and the disputed territories? Young man, can you conceive of what I have been planning here?'

The wind spun into a final guttural roar, then just as quickly died, collapsing back upon itself, until only small skirmishes of leaves remained, vague rustlings amongst the grass, and then silence. Von Ruhland stood, stock-still, staring out across the overgrown garden.

When Martin at last spoke, it was quietly, and delivered with no pretensions that his words might even be heard.

'I know you have done these things,' he said, each word cut through with hesitation. 'Things I cannot even begin to imagine. Nothing you wish is impossible. I have asked what should never have been asked. I have questioned what is unquestionable. I should never have come here. I realise that now.'

Martin looked about him, at this ruined villa on the outskirts of Potsdam. He looked at the narrow boarded windows, at the rust marks bleeding down from the iron railings – the tainted drool of an old man's mouth. He looked at the pale mottled walls, at the corrosion of the dampened brickwork, at the fallen rendering. He looked at the panelled back door, at the rusting ironwork across its glass, at the scars of lockmarks, at the wedge of leaves which pressed hard against its peeling timber, at the empty socket above.

His view moved slowly to the architect himself, who continued standing there, straight-backed, chin thrust forward.

'I'd heard about you for so long,' Martin said, the tears welling in his eyes. 'I have read. How many times? Often just the mention of your name – somebody calling upon it, a metaphor, a memory, a wish. That is all. And the traces I found. All those references. For so long. But now I have truly seen you and your works, I despise myself for these things I have done, for which I can never make amends. I weep for myself, for these others, and for us all.'

Martin straightened his jacket, pushed the ragged, wind-blown hair from his face, and with no further word turned and left the villa. He had before him a considerable walk to the station.

37

Martin changed the receiver to his other ear.

'Have you seen him?' he heard Natalie ask.

'Yes.'

She waited for him to volunteer some information.

'And how was he?' she prompted finally.

Martin hesitated. How could he say it? Eventually choosing: 'He has lost control.'

For her part, Natalie did not respond to this flat, unimpassioned statement. Perhaps she felt that it substantiated something she already believed – in any case, she did not question it, nor did she seek further clarification.

'What's happening with the Kyoto project?'

'He doesn't want it built,' Martin replied. 'He has other plans.' And he paused. 'I don't know what the council will do. Re-award it? Abandon the whole concept?'

'Are you all right?' Natalie asked. 'You don't sound well.'

'I'm okay, yes. I'm tired, that's all.'

Natalie waited a moment with the silence.

'Can I say this,' she eventually said. 'When you come back. If, *if* you need someone, I'm here. I'd like you to know that, Andrew. If you want, I'm here to help you rebuild everything – the job, your life, whatever you want.'

He thanked her. He said goodbye.

Andrew Martin left just before dawn in the hire car, the road map open on the seat beside him, driving free of Berlin with its desolate traffic. The place he sought – the name he had glimpsed that evening in Von Ruhland's apartment, enclosed in an ornately drawn rectangle at the bottom corner of the plans – had remained forever since burnt into his mind. Kranzenthal.

Before he left Germany, before he returned to what was now no longer home for him – as if any place could now fulfil that name – he needed once to see what might remain of the Cleansing Centre. The foundations, the excavations, whatever might be left. He needed to see the rooms of it, begun.

He skirted these unknown places, towns, villages, reduced to letters on *Ausfahrt* signs – Halbe, Stein, Linde. Olvenstedt, Rötha, Sauerlach – driving into the clouded autumn light.

It was not, however, as Martin had imagined it, Kranzenthal: a desolate plain, tombed with chimneys and warehouses through which a rusted railway line, its sleepers rotting back to powder, pierced its singular route onwards to the gross amphitheatre of a brown-coal quarry. What he found, nestled in a shallow valley, was a small and quite unremarkable town.

He parked the car in an outer district near a small stone church with its slate spire and its weather-vane. It was, he knew, a marker which would provide a line of sight in the face of any exploration. The traces he sought would most likely be discovered on some perimeter, the signs of which might not necessarily be those rail-tracks, those excavations, those abiding moss-ridden stones so much as the effect they'd had on the encroaching growth around and through them.

The immediate surroundings could be encompassed in a few hours. He began his slow circumambulation, bringing his feet high, stepping over the corrugations of a field, halting, staring ahead through the partly leaved trees which daubed a view – a mottle of part-near, part-distant, destroying for that instant all sense of perspective.

Soon he was within them, these thickets of pencil-trunked trees with their scribble of reddening leaves blotching the ground in half-light, half-shadow, the leafmealed earth beneath his feet muted by dampness. As soon again, the full sky washed over him. He realised he had attained the highest point of his projected journey. Below him a narrow river curved gently away, disappearing behind some outer buildings of the town. In the far distance clouds swept on their own journey, trailing rain in dark smudges along the horizon like some indigo hem.

Late afternoon found him staring once again at the field's deep corrugations. He despaired at the sight of them. Despite his fervent thoroughness, he had found no evidence of the extermination centre, no old railway lines, no foundation work, no trace of excavation.

He began a path that slowly spiralled in, moving closer to the centre of the town, crossing the river by a double-spanned stone bridge. He paused, searching for the church tower, which almost immediately announced its presence with a dull mocking ring.

The outskirts were characterised by free-standing villas, each with its terracotta roof, each with its narrow strip of garden bordered by a low hedge or a picket fence ending at the road where patches of tar met small blocks of stone. Every now and then he would sense movement at a window and would look up at the panes – the two small squares at the top and two larger rectangles below – never, though, finding a face looking back at him, only the sense of a face's disappearance.

As he moved closer to the centre of the town the houses themselves seemed to draw nearer to each other, until he found himself walking on a footpath, two persons wide, passing rows of steeply roofed half-brick, half-timbered houses.

Martin turned a street corner to find an open central square surrounded by three-storey buildings. He watched the regular procession of people crossing the cobblestones, appearing from and now disappearing down side streets, left and right, as if this were a vast stage filled with messengers.

He swung from person to person with desperate intent, seeking anyone who appeared close to Von Ruhland's age, following them, calling out his hectic, panic-filled questions in his infantile German with its ugly foreigner's pronunciation.

'*Sprechen Sie Englisch? Waren Sie hier in neunzehn zwei und vierzig?*'

He was exhausted, and this exhaustion lent an urgency to his enquiries. It was beginning to grow dark and he did not wish to stay in this place, to sleep here, lest his soul be stolen from him.

'*Ich suche die grosse Halle . . .*'

He could see people staring at him from across the square – others, closer, avoiding his eyes and veering from his path as though he were a madman, until he began to feel himself mad.

Finally it was an elderly woman who chose to speak with him. A woman dressed in a dark blue cardigan buttoned to the neck, a lighter blue skirt over thick black stockings, her hair bound in a red and white checked scarf tied beneath her chin.

'*Ich suche die grosse Halle. Kennen Sie die Todthaus?*'

'You *Englisch*?' she asked.

'Australian,' he replied.

'It is much easy for me to understand your English then your German,' she said.

Martin asked his questions, slowly forming the words and seeing the light of recognition grow steadily in her eyes.

'In 1942 they began to build a very large hall here, then the building stopped. Do you know of this?'

'You look for hall of death. Place of extermination? *Ja?*'

'*Ja*,' he said.

'You will know where the hall can be find? I'll say you where it can be find.' And she paused a moment. 'Buchholzer Strasse 18,' she said, pointing towards a distant quarter of the town.

'Not *finished*,' he said, concerned that she might have the wrong building. 'Only the beginnings can be seen.'

'*Ja*,' she answered. 'Only the beginnings.'

'*Es ist da jetzt?* It is still there now?'

'*Ja*,' said the old woman, nodding her head. 'Some things cannot be *ausradiert*.' And she made the motion of rubbing something out.

'Erased,' said Martin. 'Some things cannot be erased.'

Martin went in search of the address, trying to keep in his memory the directions he had been given, repeating over and over the slowly decreasing turns and streets like some elaborate mantra. The darkness was falling quickly now, the gaslight of the streetlamps glimmering against the dusk but still lighting no way. As he continued on this journey, the address seemed increasingly unlikely. He found himself in an old quarter of the town, walking through narrow, long-established streets. He stared at the ancient cobblestones in despair – traces of the 1940s, he well understood, would not be overlaid by sixteenth-century paving. He arrived at the address: Buchholzer Strasse 18 was an inn.

Through the small window panes he could make out various youths – rowdy, drinking, singing. He pressed himself against an adjacent wall, as he had seen people do in films, feeling that by doing this, despite logic, he could observe more freely and for longer. What needed to be seen however took only seconds to encompass. He saw the shaved heads. The colour of their shirts. He saw the armbands.

38

He returned to the Fasanenstrasse apartment, for no other reason than that it was known to him.

Anke took him in, fed him a meal which he bolted with almost doglike speed.

'What are you going to do?' she asked.

He did not know, though commonsense told him to leave this place as soon as possible.

'He is still there? At Potsdam?'

'I assume so,' she replied.

'I'm running out of money,' he said.

'If there is something to be gained by you staying on in Berlin, I have a friend, a student friend. She lives in a small flat in Prenzlauer Berg. She is away for several months. It will not be a problem for you to use it. You must understand it is very primitive – there is only a mattress, some bad chairs. There is a stove, of course. And a telephone. It is yours, this flat, for nothing; just keep a record of the power and the calls you make. There is a man upstairs, Herr Weisblum, he has the key.'

Again, there was no reason left for him to stay, other than the fact of this offer allowing him to do so. He took it as some indecipherable act of fate to which he must surrender.

Andrew Martin, suitcase in hand, left the tram at Marienburger Strasse and continued to the next street on the right. Halfway down he turned left through a large open gateway into the central courtyard of an apartment block. The buildings had clearly been rendered at some stage, but now much of the work had fallen from the bricks leaving irregular patches of colour, like a decaying poster on a billboard. A flag had been draped from a window of one apartment: '*Erst Essen! – Dann Miete.*'

Anke had told him a little about the flat, that it was

occupied by a girl named Greta on an unlimited lease for two hundred and seventy Deutschmarks a month. Its meagre space could be quickly explored. In the main room there were the bad chairs, a small table and the mattress, its bedding still in a state of disarray. There was a wardrobe half full of women's clothes, and a small chest of drawers containing various out-of-date medicines, underwear, pieces of cheap jewellery. The room's only decoration was an unfolded map of Berlin which had been stuck to one of the walls. The second room was a combined kitchen and bathroom. A tin tub had been placed beside a window, the bottom part of which had been covered by newspaper. The toilet, he had learned from Herr Weisblum, was on the landing below, a small, low-ceilinged room at the turn of the stair. From the top of the kitchen window he saw the other flats, their exterior walls holding little more of the rendering than his own. He looked down on the near-bare chestnut tree in the central courtyard.

That evening, a woman in her late fifties came to the door holding two empty buckets.

'*Ich komme wegen Wasser,*' she said. '*Keine Umstände, ich hol' es mir selber.*'

She moved past Martin and walked straight to the kitchen where she filled the two buckets with water.

'*Vielen Dank,*' she said as she moved back through the door. '*Wir sehen uns sicher morgen. Bis dann.*'

Martin understood barely a word, beyond the fact that something would happen tomorrow.

Shortly before ten o'clock, a young man called. He looked at Martin suspiciously.

'*Greta. Ist Greta zu Hause?*'

'*Nein,*' Martin began. '*Es ist nicht hier. Zwei* . . .' And he realised he did not have the word for 'month'. '*Acht Woche,*' he replied.

Several days passed, the passage of time measured by the nightly arrival of the woman with the water buckets. Martin increasingly began to question the purpose of staying. If fate had decreed he was to remain in Berlin, he could see no reason for it. Certainly, though, he did not want to leave the city with the image of Von Ruhland as he had seen him at Potsdam. He needed the telephone to ring, or a letter to be pushed again under his door, reassuring him that all would return to how it was. And then he began to wonder if that state had ever existed in reality. Or was it rather a construction of the older architect's, or simply a misreading of his own?

He walked the streets. He saw the scar traces of the Wall, these absences threading through the city. He found the abandoned beginnings of Zumthor's 'Topography of Terror': two staircases leading to nothing, a vast absent centre. The only semblance of his modelling were the weed-infested piles of rubble. From four o'clock he watched the unrelenting stream of pedestrians skirting the construction sites along planked corridors stained with drying mud, heads down, deadened to the rise of building after building from the earth around them. He saw a vast accumulation of smaller cities, themselves constantly in a state of flux. He saw that, ultimately, none of this could possibly be explained by his stranger's eyes, even without the distortions of his melancholia. It was rather as if the city stood there making its endless evaluations of him, this pitiful creature crawling pointlessly around a design he could never encompass. A thing that might be crushed without so much as a thought.

The time arrived when to remain became senseless, when shame was less a burden than anonymity. This moment of decision to leave, to return to Melbourne, was followed almost instantly by a reason to remain. That same night, shortly before ten o'clock, Martin received a phone call from Anke.

'Hello,' he said. 'I've been meaning to ring you. I've decided to return to Australia. I'm going to get a flight back sometime later this week. I'll return the key to Herr Weisblum.'

Her words cut into the pause.

'He's dying.'

'What do you mean?' asked Martin, a sense of panic already rising in him, the blood rushing from his hands, his skin prickling.

'Every day he grows weaker. He refuses to eat.'

'How long has this been going on?'

'Since last week. He came back here from Potsdam, broken. He has totally turned in on himself. He talks only of how you defeated him. Of how you had replaced him because of what you said and what you did not say.' She took a deep breath. 'What *did* you say to him?'

'I hardly said a thing. It was Johannes who spoke to *me*.'

She waited a moment, as if contemplating the significance of what he'd said.

'Tonight he was calling for you,' she began. 'Repeating your name over and over. You must come now.'

Martin glanced at his watch.

'If you feel for him as I think only you do, you must come. Only you can help him. He will not listen to me. There is no-one else he can turn to.'

'All right,' he agreed. 'Just give me a couple of minutes to get ready. I'll get a cab – do you know a number to call?'

'26 1026,' she said instantly. 'Tell them it's *dringend*.'

39 Martin waited on the footpath for the taxi to arrive. Across the road was a substantial red-brick building which he knew, from the passage of children he had seen go to and from it, as a school, but which the map stuck upon the wall of Greta's apartment had told him was a hospital. A tram, sliding past the street's-end glimpse of Prenzlauer Allee, caught his attention, its brightly lit interior come and gone within a second or two, like the blink of some behemoth. He turned up his collar, thrust his hands deep into the pockets of his coat.

The front door was unlocked.

'Hello,' he called, stepping inside. 'Hello? Anke?'

Martin moved slowly through room after room. He

pushed open the door to the living room to find the carpet had been rolled away again, the furniture once more moved to the walls. He listened to his footfall on the polished floorboards. He stepped to the far door and crossed the dining room, past the central table, his hand coming to rest on the doorknob. He turned it slowly, knowing how the door gave directly onto the passageway and to the mirror at the passage's end.

As if to surprise whatever he felt made its home in the glass – there was no other explanation – he suddenly flung the door wide. There, where his own image should have been, he found the shape of Von Ruhland – stooped, bent by some invisible burden – staring back at him.

'Andrew,' the image called, and walked forward holding out its arms. Martin's heart pounded fitfully, a fist beating at a locked door.

Only the slightest glimpse behind the approaching figure of its own back reflected in the mirror's surface restored the sanity to this place.

'My beloved Andrew,' he said. 'Is it you? Have you sought me here?'

He moved closer and reached out his hand to touch Martin's cheek.

'My love,' he said. 'You have returned to me in the face of my acts and my words. You have come here, my beloved servant, humbling me.'

Martin felt the coldness of the architect's hand upon him – the touch, he imagined, of the dead.

'How I am blessed!' Von Ruhland said. 'You have come

where all others would have cursed me and all of my work. Please, help me to a chair. I must talk with you.'

Andrew took him by the arm and led him back into the living room. He helped the architect to one of the chairs arranged around the walls.

'Anke has been here, by the look of things,' Von Ruhland said, gesturing to the cleared space.

'She's not here now?'

'Not to my knowledge. Now, bring a chair for yourself – yes, closer.'

Von Ruhland lowered his voice almost to a whisper.

'Do not think your acts have gone unnoticed. Your courage, your integrity, your respect. And your subjection.' He smiled. 'My dear Andrew, how beautiful you are, so perfect and upright. Nothing causes you to cower. Your love and your faith are so absolute.'

Von Ruhland motioned Martin to come even closer; the young architect could feel the older man's breath upon his face.

'After you left the villa, after hearing your words, I suddenly felt our greatnesses reversed. What is this frail morality, I thought, that causes mine to crumble? That reduces all my works so far to some rococo obscenity?'

Martin kept his head perfectly still and stared out into the room. He saw the clutter of furniture clinging to the periphery, and the empty centre, the boards laid bare, exposed.

'You never failed to love me, did you Andrew? Tell me that now. Tell me.'

Martin turned to face Von Ruhland.

'*Ich liebe dich,*' he said.

Von Ruhland took Martin's head in his hands and brought their mouths together.

'*Ja!*' he cried, breaking from the kiss, his whole manner strangely invigorated. 'You are mine forever.'

The telephone on its table in the very corner of the room began to ring. Andrew made a tentative move towards it.

'Let it ring,' said Von Ruhland. 'Nothing could be as important as your presence here.'

The older architect waited till the ringing stopped.

'Now,' he said, 'I have some things to tell you. Please bear with me. First, I have decided that my wealth – my property, my investments, my belongings – shall be equally divided between yourself and Anke –'

'Johannes, no, I don't want these things,' Martin began. But the older architect brought his finger to his lips to silence him.

'And my various plans, the sketches and designs shall be passed on to you alone.'

Martin began another protest, once again to be silenced.

'I will hear no argument against this. You cannot begin to understand your significance. You have become like a son to me.'

He placed his hand on the young architect's arm.

'Andrew, you have given me another life, one that I thought had been lost forever.'

Martin was uncertain what to say, but into that silence of indecision he heard Von Ruhland continuing.

'Come close,' he was saying, his voice barely audible. 'I need you to do this one thing for me. Tonight, though. It must be done tonight. You will help me in this regard?'

'Of course,' said Martin, but there was trepidation in his heart.

Von Ruhland stood and made his way determinedly to the mantelpiece. More of his strength seemed to have returned, his posture had regained a measure of its uprightness. On the ledge, propped against the porcelain figurine, was a twice-folded sheet of writing paper. Von Ruhland took it in his hand and returned to the chair.

'You must go to the other side of Berlin. To this address.' He took a fountain pen from his pocket and wrote some words on the front of the piece of paper. 'You must give this note to those who live there. You must take the U15 line from Uhlandstrasse to Schlesisches Tor. Once you have left the station, you will need more specific instructions. I will give them to you now.'

Martin watched as Von Ruhland hastily sketched out a nest of streets like some spiderish ideogram. Against several of the strokes he wrote abbreviated names in a miniature script. When he had finished, he screwed the top back on his pen and replaced it in his pocket. He leant forward with the folded paper in his hand. Martin saw for the first time that the note had been sealed with wax.

'Schlesisches Tor Station is here,' he said, indicating a line at the top of the sketch in which an eyelet shape had been drawn. 'And here,' he pointed again, this time to a cross marked at the furthest distance from the station, 'here is your destination.'

40

Martin set off into the darkness. It seemed in some ways more familiar to him than the other city, this *Berlin bei Nacht* – the light gathering to its accustomed places, surrounding the tops of the ornate poles or trapped in the frames of scattered windows, high, unreachable, above the street, the white dress and fair hair of it, pining for dispersion. Now he saw how it was scooped from the air and funnelled in an increasingly blinding accumulation by the grilles of passing cars.

He was this solitary walker meandering through the streets of the city, seeing everything with wonder as if for a first and a last time. Intermingling surprise with loss. Here he saw light hung in strips high above the road, here in circles stained with amber.

He turned into Ku'damm. The boulevard lay before him like a vast factory, processing raw light into recognisable, usable shapes, sometimes extinguished and reignited in patterns – moulds filled with the stuff, forming sequences of letters. On the wide pavements outside buildings men stood calling to passers-by, promising rooms filled with it, thick to the touch. Ahead he could see light pasted over the demolished spire of Kaiser Wilhelm Church, a fine spray of its whiteness escaping into the air above.

Martin took a seat beside a window, facing the direction of the train. The glass next to him was badly defaced, scratched with meaningless initials: BOR, SYK, ROK, ZAR, KZS.

The train pulled out from Uhlandstrasse. In front of him a handful of passengers sat in the cruel illumination of the carriage. At Möckernbrücke a young man entered, pacing the aisle back and forth: a single ranting man, a pamphlet in his hand, seeking to convince his audience, at least one of whom was unable to speak the tongue of his explication, of some grievance, some injustice. And so these carriages, these people, this small alley of day continued to be hurtled through the realm of darkness.

By Martin's stop the carriage was empty. He stepped alone from the train onto a platform empty in both directions. He looked for the closest *Ausgang* sign and headed for the steps.

Now, in this distant quarter, the light gathered in impoverished patches: here above this solitary woman leaning at the station entrance, here briefly glowing at the face of a passing smoker. Only a few streetlamps appeared in the near distance, their soft gaslight dispersing in a haze to the night air. Beyond, there seemed only darkness.

He walked on until he came to a set of steps leading upwards to an unlit park. He continued along what was now a wide path bordered by open ground. Should he have turned before here? The small map already seemed insufficient. He decided he must soon turn left in order to make some compensation. This led him to the edge of a canal. He brought his face close to the piece of paper. Were these parallel lines the canal or one of the streets either side of it? He crossed at a small footbridge, following the street to which it led for some metres, then decided he would turn left. He stopped and stared about him – the paths had begun to multiply, their names unrevealed. He looked down the narrow street before him, the buildings rising up almost from the roadway. A canyon.

Martin's heart began to pound, his mouth became dry. The best thing, he began to tell himself, would be to return. Ahead was only danger. Ahead was chaos. It was hardly unforgivable that the note not be delivered this night, but some eight or nine hours later instead. What, in all probability, would the older architect know of the difference anyway? But then he could not tell how crucial Von Ruhland's message might be. Besides, had he not promised Johannes this thing would be done now? He had no right to question what he did not know, even if the whole thing struck him as increasingly ludicrous.

These thoughts had taken his mind from deciphering the way. He was, he realised, hopelessly lost, unaware of how many streets or lanes he had passed, or indeed whether these were here upon the map, and finally unsure even of the direction in which he was now walking. He decided in the circumstances that he must move to the place of most light, wherever it might be. He would regather there. He would find street names, he would restore his bearings and endeavour to mount one final attempt. Martin turned the corner into a narrow roadway running alongside another canal.

It was not long after that he saw them – a slowly moving barrier of six or seven young men stretched from the building walls across to the bank of the canal. Perhaps, it came to him in that straw-clutch of desperation, the message was for them. He took the letter paper in his hand, broke the wax seal and unfolded it. The page was blank.

The young architect walked slowly, but with no hesitation, towards them. He offered them his frailty, his creativity, his speechlessness, his obedience; he offered even a type of halting, blemished faithfulness. He brought these things in innocence.

He came to a halt, listening to the malicious laughter turning into anger, seeded by itself. He heard a word similar to that which had been used by the prostitute the night of the Biennale. He heard the words *Tunte* and *Arschficker*.

He knew that to flee was pointless. He saw their physiques, each far more powerful than his. Any one of them, he knew, would run him to ground.

The first blow broke his nose, blinding him with tears. His hands rushed to his face, Von Ruhland's note falling to the street, tumbling to a gutter, softly turned by a brief gust of wind, planing its way onwards, finally lost to view. As he spun away in pain, a second blow, a fist hitting him in the nape of the neck, brought him down to the cobbled street. Then the boots were at his body.

The seventh and the eighth kick had been enough to

damage him irreparably, but the business continued until one had withdrawn to catch his breath and another took this as a sign to cease, a sign to leave this curled and bloodied thing where it was.

And so the thought passed without word through the rest of them and they turned and walked hurriedly from this place with perfect anonymity.

epilogue

Anke came through the front door. In her hand she carried Martin's suitcase, containing all he had brought with him to Berlin this final time.

She moved through the apartment straight to the living room, where she stood, her eyes taking in Von Ruhland seated against the far wall next to the telephone. She placed the suitcase on the floorboards directly in front of him.

'*Danke schön,*' he said.

Anke walked up to the architect and gently kissed him on the forehead.

'*Gute Nacht, meine Liebe,*' he said.

'*Gute Nacht,*' she replied and silently, without footfall, retired to her room.

Von Ruhland waited a few minutes, then rose from the chair. He laid the suitcase down, pressed the clasps and lifted the lid. Inside were many things he remembered from the young architect's stay – a familiar shirt, the pullover whose sleeves forever needed pushing back. And other things which he had never seen – a notebook with some naïve sketches for buildings, a packet of Gauloises Blondes, a small, off-white feather.

Von Ruhland closed the lid and placed the suitcase up against the wall. He exited the living room and moved through the dining room, down the passageway towards the mirror.

'It is over?' came the question.

'Yes.'

'It will be better now. You did what you had to.'

Von Ruhland replied slowly.

'I believe, just before the end, he had a brief moment of doubt, an understandable fear that he had been forsaken, but he was able to surrender to it.'

'You loved each other.'

'*Völlig*,' said Von Ruhland, and then added, 'but I now know this – that until one learns to love oneself, one cannot love others.'

So saying, he moved from view of the mirror, his reflection splitting from him. He walked to the window of his study and threw it wide. A music came to him, the hum of late evening traffic. And it seemed that on the wind was the sound of distant construction work. There was a new city to be built beneath a black sky, beneath the stars.

Acknowledgments

I would like to thank Professors Gerard Sutton and Sharon Bell of the University of Wollongong and Professor Masaaki Tatsuki of Doshisha University, Kyoto, for the support they have given to this project. Thanks are also due to the Literature Board of the Australia Council for a New Work grant.

The following people gave generously of their time and energy: in Kyoto, Hiroshi Funamoto and Mazza Kanaya; in Berlin, Raoul Bunschoten of Chora Institute of Architecture and Urbanism, Gerrit Confurius from Daidalos, Julia Harmon, Doctor Ralf Melzer (Director, Anti-Defamation Forum), Jochen Paul, Silke Ramelow and Michael Schmidt; in Australia, John Garnett, John Hawke, Jill Jones, Robin Lucas, Julie Marlow, Helen Moore, Meredith Rose and Andrew Scollo.

I am indebted to certain aspects of the argument of Jung's *Answer to Job*, and to the remarkable translation of and commentary on The Book of Job undertaken by David Wolfers in *Deep Things Out of Darkness*.

Material on pages 6–7 from Peter Zumthor's *Three Concepts* is used with permission of the publisher: Edition Architekturgalerie Luzern, Birkhäuser Verlag, Basel, Switzerland, 1997.

Elizabeth Francis and John Hughes have been with this project from the beginning, offering help, encouragement and good ideas. This book is for them.